Enimnori

CHALLENGE

ENIMNORI SERIES
BOOK THREE

JEFF WEBBER

Lewis Publications

Copyright

Dedication

This book is dedicated to my family and friends (in particular my "big sister" Susie) for considerable encouragement and a lot of valuable feedback.

Reviews

"I rate this book 4 out of 4 stars… Enimnori: Arrival can be enjoyed by everyone who likes complex and intricate stories that are also easy to follow and understand."

— OnlineBookClub.org

"…a suspenseful adventure with the main characters Scott Hathaway, and Brandon, –whose magic and skills bring them to the battlefield determining the best course of action…"

— Diane Calabrese MS, CTRS-professor/author of Mind, Body, Spirit and Discovering the Purpose of Life

"I was sort of reminded of Yankee in King Arthur's Court with this one in a way as it was really fun to see

Scott use his modern knowledge to influence the battle of a Medieval-type society. It was going the other way too, and exploring Webber's world of magic and sorcerers' battle"

— Joshua Grant (DiabolicShrimp.com)

The story up to now:

BOOK ONE

A man from the modern world, Scott Hathaway, an electronics engineer with a penchant for martial arts, and medieval reenactments, gets accidentally transported to another world where magic is real. In the course of learning their language and customs he becomes friends with his accidental summoner, a powerful, but very young magician named Brandon, and his teacher, master magician Morgan. The two magicians become embroiled in a battle to protect their home from an ambitious Baron, who was planning an attack with overwhelming force. Scott, not wanting to see his new friends killed or enslaved, teaches them how to make gunpowder and the weapons that use it, thus saving their home. Grateful, they organize an expedition to find more of the "special crystals" that enhance their power, in an attempt to send him back to his own world and family.

BOOK TWO

Upon passing through the "Wild Zone" and arriving at Dead Lake, near the mountain that is the only known source of the crystals, they discover that Dead Lake is a crater caused by a nuclear war during which the original settlers of this world destroyed their own civilization, the remnants going in two directions. Most of them became hunters and farmers, discovered magic, and have gradually built a new civilization (where Scott first found himself), roughly the equivalent of Europe during the Middle Ages. The smaller group survived in an underground city near the site of the crater, where they have lived ever since, while their technology slowly breaks down around them. The group finds out that their original troubles were caused by the leader of the underground society who was seeking to expand his influence outward. After Scott is able to use knowledge from his world to help repair some of their broken technology, they join with a resistance movement, and help bring about a change to a more peaceful government. They secretly gather some of the crystals and return home after setting up a diplomatic relationship with the new regime. During their adventures on the homeward journey they find out that Scott is actually a magician (although obviously he never knew it), and decide to teach him to use his newfound abilities as the first step in finding a way to send him home.

Map of the Enimnori Continent

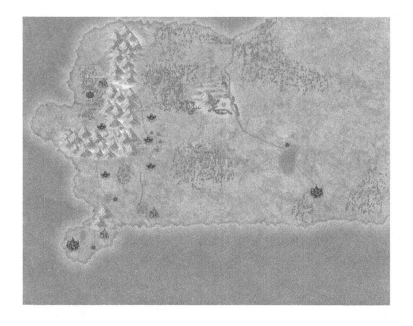

CHAPTER

One

Scott Hathaway stared glumly at the waxed paper cylinder with the flickering candle inside. As thrilling as it was to know that he could do real magic, it was a little frustrating. *I can do this stuff, but I'm pretty weak compared to the others.* His best effort so far had reduced the air pressure inside the wax cylinder only enough to make the candle burn out in about 13 minutes instead of 15 (¼ mark as these people counted time). Shaking his head to clear it, he flicked a quick glance at Morgan, working in the corner, and then shifted his attention to the trio of small, lead musket balls on the table. They all rose into the air gracefully and began spinning around his head, moving around each other in a complex, rhythmic dance. *THIS I can do just fine...better than Brandon, even...can't move near as much though. I wonder what else....*

"STUDENT!"

The balls froze in place, then lowered to the table. He

sighed, and turned his attention to Morgan again. "Yes sir?"

"STUDENT'S DO NOT –" Seeing Scott meeting his gaze steadily, Morgan reminded himself that this was no ordinary student, but a highly accomplished...engineer... a word, and concept, that had only recently been introduced to his people (by Scott himself). Taking a deep breath, he continued. "I know it can be frustrating, but please try to focus on the assignment."

Sighing, Scott focused on the cylinder again. After a minute, he had a sudden thought. Since movement seemed to be his thing, maybe...he took a deep, slow, cleansing breath and began trying to visualize oxygen moving out through the paper and nitrogen moving in. When he got that still-strange feeling of readiness, he gave the mental 'execute' command. About 15 or 20 seconds later, the flame flickered a couple of times and winked out. He chuckled happily, inadvertently catching his teacher's attention again.

Morgan glanced at the cylinder, then did a sharp double take, his eyes widening. He rose to his feet, walked slowly across the room, and concentrated briefly. His eyes widened even further. He raised the cylinder slightly, and looked at the candle before putting it back down carefully. He stepped back. "There was no pressure difference. What did you do?"

Scott tried to explain. "When the pressure thing didn't seem to be working, I thought I would try replacing the oxygen inside the cylinder with nitrogen from the outside," he said somewhat sheepishly. "I know that's not exactly what you said, but the effect is basically the same, and it...." he paused, wondering how to express it. "Well, it somehow felt more natural for me."

Morgan was torn between anger at being disobeyed and the warm feeling of having a student figure something out for himself. The warm feeling won. "I'm not sure I fully understand, but it does seem to have worked well." He stopped to think, reminding himself, for what seemed like the thousandth time, that this was no ordinary student. He looked out the window at the Day Sphere lowering in the western sky. *What does Scott call it...the sun? That word still seems strange.* "Why don't you run...I mean would you please go to the market and get us some supper?" Receiving a nod, he returned to his desk, and sat, deep in thought as Scott left. He considered the situation carefully. *It has only been three months, but this just doesn't feel right...I have to keep reminding myself that this is NOT an ordinary student, but a grown man...a professional who isn't even really familiar with our ways yet. He's way beyond student level in so many ways, but I can't promote him yet...or can I?* The more he thought about it, the more reasonable it seemed. Not only did Scott already have a better grasp of control and meditation than most Journeymen (and even a few Elites Morgan could think of), but given his previous accomplishments and special status... Morgan chuckled to himself. *Given the rumors I doubt anyone would dare to complain...* He frowned. *At least not openly. Even if they do, certainly Wesley would approve.* While a promotion from Student to Journeyman was unheard of, Morgan knew in his heart that Apprentice status would be just as bad, and damn it, the man was worthy. Smiling to himself, he squared his shoulders, took out a piece of paper, and began to write.

Scott walked toward the market place lost in thought. As usual it was teeming with activity. Most of the vendors simply erected tents to house their wares, with only a select few having permanent wooden buildings. Sadly some of those were still empty following the purges of the late, unlamented Baron Harkness.

The well in the center of the square was the center of its own hive of activity, with city dwellers as well as the vendors filling buckets. Glancing at the two guards following discreetly behind him, Scott mused, *they bugged the hell out of me at first, but everybody insisted...and you know, they've become friends, and now I would miss them if they weren't there.* He felt the warmth of the sun on his shoulders and smiled. He sighed, *I guess I'm going to have to try and act more humble and obedient in front of Morgan. He's trying, but I can tell it bugs him when I'm not subservient. It grates on me, but what the hell? I really do respect the man tremendously, and I do want to learn as much as I can.* He wondered glumly how long he would have to put up with it. *I don't know how long the student thing lasts, but I seem to remember that apprenticeships can last for years, and from what Brandon said, that might even be worse!* Oh well, everything he learned would hopefully bring him one step closer to going home, or at least somehow being able to tell them he was okay.

"Scott!" A familiar voice brought him out of his reverie. He looked around. "Winston! Hi, it's good to see you.

How is your arm?" Several months ago, Winston, the ambassador from Landbelow, the last remnant of technological civilization in this world, had taken an arrow in the shoulder, one that had been aimed at Scott.

"Better, thank you." Winston slowly raised his arm to shoulder level, wincing slightly.

"That's a lot better than it was! How are you getting along with Count Wesley?" *Wow! That arm has really healed well! I wonder if Morgan or one of his friends had a hand in that?*

The man nodded carefully (Winston tended to do most things carefully). "I would say quite well. We are attempting to decide what items would be most useful for trade and have tentatively scheduled a return trip in about 3 more months. How are your studies going?"

Scott shrugged. "Kind of slow. It's not really easy being treated like a student, even though the material is quite...ah...interesting."

One of Winston's guards coughed, and pointedly looked at the sun. "I'm sorry, I am expected at the castle. I almost forgot, Mason asked if he could meet you in the market about noon tomorrow. Would you care to respond?"

"Why yes, would you please tell him...that would be acceptable," Scott answered gravely.

"Very well. I wish you well and hope to see you again soon." He bowed stiffly and walked away, leaving Scott grinning at his back. *He has certainly changed! He was such a prissy, stiff-necked xenophobe, and now look at him!* He almost laughed at remembering how the man had almost gotten himself lynched by trying to have the hunters guarding the caravan shine their shoes and march in a straight line through the forest on the way back from Dener Peak. Shaking his head and glancing at the guards, he suddenly realized he had forgotten to activate the spell that enabled him to sense moods. *Crap! I keep forgetting that spell! I really should get used to doing it when I go out in public, even if just for practice.* He carefully yawned hugely and stretched to hide the gestures. Speaking the necessary words under his breath, he became aware of an undercurrent of feelings surrounding him. Embarrassingly, several people were surreptitiously regarding him with awe, and a little fear, while one young woman...blushing slightly, he hastily withdrew from that direction, and, smiling at his guards, continued on his way. Trying to distract himself from the young woman who seemed to be fantasizing about him, he focused as closely as he could in the other direction, and, just to make things harder, he ratcheted up his hearing as well. *As much as I don't like eavesdropping, I really need to practice, ESPECIALLY at doing multiple things at once. That still tends to give me headaches!*

He stumbled slightly, and recovered with a mild curse. *Oh great! Now I'm tripping over pebbles in the street!* He forced himself to stay aware of his surroundings while still concentrating, and began to sweat, despite the coolness of the afternoon. He slowed his walk. *What the heck is that?* Stopping at a random booth, he lowered his head as if examining the items on the table in front of him, and tried to tune out his surroundings entirely. THERE...off to the right. There was no anger, or aggression, but something was wrong. Someone was subvocalizing *"the wind is blowing quietly through the forest"* over and over again, like a mantra of some kind. He blinked and glanced over, expecting to see someone meditating, but just saw the thinning crowd swirling around the vendor's tables. *Why would somebody be...*something clicked in his mind. *DAMN, this is too much like those people in the forest when Brandon was kidnapped.* He stiffened and his head snapped around, eyes searching the crowd. *They MUST have been trained to think of something calm so as not to trip the 'threat detection' spell.* The mantra stopped instantly, and suddenly he sensed shock, followed by annoyance mixed with fear. There was a stirring in the crowd, and the feeling faded. John and Karg, his two guards, stiffened, hands reaching for weapons, as they saw him react. He shook his head slightly and gave the 'okay' hand signal. John stepped forward quickly and grabbed his arm to steady him as he wavered and almost fell. "What is it?" he asked quietly. "Are you alright?"

Scott took a couple of deep breaths. "Yeah, sorry, I must be tired or something. I just got a little dizzy for a minute there. I think I'm okay now." The two of them eyed him narrowly, sensing that something was up, but having been warned that their charge was often involved with things it was better not to know about, they kept their silence, but remained wary.

He had originally been going to pick up some fruit and a couple of vegetables, but the enticing aroma of stew and fresh bread had been too much to resist, and he had, almost unconsciously, gone in that direction. Now standing at the small tavern that served the finest stew in Enimnori, he gave in and bought two bowls of stew and a loaf of fresh bread before heading back, stopping only briefly to buy a bag of apples as well.

The two of them were eating the bread and stew when Morgan said warily, "John said you had some kind of problem at the market. What happened?"

"Yeah, I did want to talk to you about that. I was practicing sensing, and was doing the enhanced hearing thing at the same time..." Morgan eyebrows went up slightly. "And I caught someone trying to hide their emotions. When I turned to look, I lost my balance a bit and stumbled. That's probably what he meant, but anyway, when the person in question realized that I noticed what he or she was doing, they got frightened and left," he said tightly. "It made me think of the ambush when Brandon was kidnapped."

Morgan said slowly, "I can see why it would and, while it may be nothing, you may have saved us a lot of trouble. Good job. Now, you don't usually go around losing your balance. Is there something else I should know about?"

Scott sighed. "Yes, I got weak and dizzy when I used both spells at the same time. I guess my magic...strength still leaves something to be desired," he said somewhat dejectedly.

Morgan almost looked angry. "Scott, I think you still have skewed notions about magical strength from being around Brandon so much. Please remember that he is EXTREMELY powerful, and you shouldn't judge yourself in comparison." He stroked his beard for a second. "Actually, that does bring up another topic I want to discuss with you." He glared at Scott for a moment, then chuckled. "In light of your progress so far, I am declaring your Student stage to be at an end. I sent the papers to the guild today." He held up his hand as Scott started to speak. "Furthermore, in one week, you will be promoted to Journeyman." He sighed. "In all fairness, you probably should have started as an advanced apprentice to begin with, for which I apologize."

Scott was stunned. "Are you sure this won't cause bad feelings or something? I can live with this for a while if needed. You've been very understanding," he said ruefully. "I do realize that this situation has been hard for you as well."

"No, I've thought about it, and given your age and advanced meditation skill, anyone who dares to complain can...how did you say it once...'go suck an egg'?" Morgan grinned broadly, rose and held out his hand. "Congratulations. Just don't say anything about the Journeyman thing till next week when we have the official ceremony. You can take off the Student hat and armband immediately."

Scott rose, took Morgan's hand, and said warmly, "Thank you." He hesitated. "I know you think we have too many projects going as it is, but I have something that's been on my mind for quite a while...."

Morgan looked at him sourly, then suddenly burst out laughing. "I had a feeling that I might regret making you a Journeyman, but I didn't think it would be before you were actually promoted. After next week, there isn't much to keep you from working on whatever you want to, so go ahead, give me your idea. What bizarre subtlety of the way things work are we going to exploit now?" He couldn't seem to stop laughing. "Are we to levitate the Count's castle to the top of the cliff, or build something to find the best spot for growing apples? No wait, you want to create something so that one of your telescopes will keep watching one of the moons all by itself, as the moon moves across the sky...."

Scott couldn't help but laugh as well. "You know that might not be all that hard...there's something called a servo motor...."

This set Morgan off again. "Argh! Save me from the monster I have created!" After several minutes he managed to stop, and wiped his eyes. "By the powers, I haven't laughed that hard for a long time. Thank you my weird and wonderful friend!" He sighed heavily. "I might as well hear it."

"Well, in my world we discovered some properties of crystals that make them useful in long range communication. Basically, electricity makes them vibrate, and if you physically vibrate THEM, then you GET electricity. Anyway, if we have two crystals that vibrate at the same frequency, or rate, then I believe we can use them as endpoints for the electromagnetic equivalent of our 'telephone' system, then we come up with a way to turn the EM into sound and vice versa."

There was a long pause, "Is this more of that 'light we cannot see' business?"

"Pretty much, yes." Scott said slowly, "You made the radioactivity detectors, and the gizmo that turned out to be a door opener in Landbelow. Do you think…?" He stopped as Morgan began to scowl. "Okay, okay, I know you're busy. Could you show me how to do that?

Morgan stared at him in shock. "Sure, if you want to spend years learning the principles, no problem, no problem at all," he said acidly. He held up his hand as Scott started to speak. "Before I commit to anything just what kind of distance are we talking about?"

Scott chewed his lip before answering. "I…can't promise anything and… it may need line of sight, but it may not, depending on –"

Morgan snapped, "Look, I'm not asking for your first born here, and I promise not to have you arrested if you're wrong." Seeing Scott still hesitate, he sighed. "Okay just tell me how it works in your world. What's the farthest this…whatever…has ever worked?"

"Well, under the right conditions, you can talk to someone on the other side of the world, and this is the same principle used to communicate with spacecraft that are so far away. I don't even know how to say it in your language."

Morgan got very still. "So…if this works right we could talk with Varney in Landbelow, three months travel away!"

"Yes, but there are a lot of –"

Morgan held up his hand again. "Spare me, I'm not asking for promises. Well, you DEFINITELY have my attention! We will start the day AFTER your promotion ceremony." He glanced at the growing darkness outside.

"I'm going to turn in early, and you might want to do the same. What were you going to do tomorrow?"

"I was going to try working on recharging that battery again. I ran into Winston at the market and he said Geon wants to meet for lunch tomorrow and that reminded me."

Morgan nodded. "We'll work on that first thing then. Good night."

"Good night."

The two men met the following morning in Morgan's lab. Scott smiled as he entered. *I like this place.* Everything from the row of work tables along one wall to the modest bookcases flanking the small, stone fireplace at one end felt comfortable, even though it could have been a bit gloomy (being an inside room with no windows). The series of candles mounted on the walls somehow made it homey instead. The group of shelves and storage cabinets reminded him of his own workshop back home, even though some of the contents were truly bizarre.

After starting a small fire in the fireplace (it was still a bit chilly), they got to work. Walking over to the workbench, Scott carefully placed the battery they had borrowed from the technologically advanced, but decaying society in the underground city of Landbelow on the workbench. Scott began trying to explain to Morgan what they were trying to do. "In general, there is a chemical reaction that takes place inside. If you connect something that uses electrical power to the terminals...." He pointed to the metal stubs projecting from the end, "Then, what we call electrons flow from this one to that one, providing power." He paused, running his hands through his hair.

He had already tried, without success, to explain atomic structure to both Morgan and Brandon. Unfortunately, their backgrounds were so different from his, that for once he had failed. He continued somewhat dejectedly. "What we are trying to do now is force the electrons to flow in the opposite direction, and...uh...make the reaction run in reverse, kind of like winding...um..." Remembering that they hadn't invented clocks yet, he floundered to a halt. "Ah...okay, kind of like refilling a lake above a stream where you have a water wheel. So it can flow back down."

Morgan said slowly, "I get the waterwheel concept...I think, but I can't picture the elect...?"

"Electron."

"Okay, electron business." Morgan frowned. "Perhaps you can visualize it, and I can simply supply power."

Scott took a deep breath. "Okay." Carefully trying to picture the electrons running backwards into the battery, he felt Morgan's support, like a hand helping him lift something, and it seemed to be working, but after more than an hour the charge indicator was still the same red it had always been. Scott finally sat down, his head in his hands. "This is so frustrating! It feels like it's working, but nothing happens." He sighed, then looked out the window. "I guess it's almost time for me to meet Geon at the market." He looked at Morgan guiltily. "Sorry, I wasted your time."

Morgan waved away his apology. "Most of your ideas have been very useful." He smiled slightly, "If we had to fail at something, at least it was this, and not making cannons or gunpowder. Go visit your friend and try to relax." Looking Scott in the eye he said ruefully, "You look kind of beat. You're probably not going to be able to do much for the rest of the day. Have a good afternoon, and bring something back for supper."

Scott sighed heavily, and stood up slowly, "All right, see you later."

A short while later Scott was seated at the Hillview Tavern with Geon Mason, while two not so unobtrusive guards lounged at a nearby table, and two more were randomly browsing the nearby vendors. This time Scott had remembered to cast the emotion sensor spell before leaving Morgan's house, and so was aware of the 'emotional currents' in the tavern and the surrounding market area. He noticed that Geon was uncomfortable. A moment later he sensed with dismay that Geon was afraid of him! In shock, he probed a little deeper, and saw that instead of fear, per se, it was more like awe. He took a few sips of beer to hide his discomfort, then said quickly, "I wonder how Brandon is doing? I think that caravan is due back in a few days, isn't it?"

Geon smiled, relaxing somewhat. "Yes, I believe so. It'll be good to see him again. There's not a lot of people here I can talk to."

Scott grunted sympathetically, "Yeah, that I can understand." He sighed. "I am sorry to report that we STILL can't seem to recharge your battery. I thought for sure I'd be able to make it work, but...." He shrugged and spread his hands helplessly.

Geon chuckled. "Well, no offense intended, but, to be honest, I never really believed it would work, so I can't say

I'm upset. Thank you for trying." He regarded his glass thoughtfully. "Most of your food is pretty good, but, as long as I'm being honest, your beer leaves something to be desired."

Scott burst out laughing. "Sorry...sorry. Hey, maybe you can get a job at a brewery. That would be a kick! Geon the ambassador and brew master!"

Geon laughed as well. "It's good to know I have something to fall back on." He shook with renewed mirth. "Hey, it beats what I used to do!"

Scott roared, tears streaming down his face. "I would say that your previous job as a shoveler of animal feces prepared you very well for your position as an ambassador!"

Geon was shaking slightly. "Why, yes I CAN shovel it with the best of them! My position is secure! CHEERS!" They knocked their mugs together and drained them. "HAH! Two more!"

Two hours later a somewhat tipsy Scott waved goodbye to an even tipsier Geon, and the two of them walked off unsteadily, their amused guards following behind them.

CHAPTER
Two

FOUR MEN (TWO ARMED) FINISHED CLIMBING THE STAIRS, walked down the dusty corridor, and entered the cave, roughly square, about 30 or 40 feet on a side with complex equipment arrayed along the side walls. Those on the right had been badly damaged by a rock fall. However, on the left side of the room, a few small lights could still be dimly seen on several complicated control panels. The further wall appeared to be natural stone, with the exception of an open recessed door set somewhat off-center. Two of the men sighed, and putting on work gloves, began shifting stones (after much discussion, the leadership had decided to clear the wreckage).

Glancing at the other two, one of them muttered under his breath, "Gee, isn't it great we have them to guard us while we work?" Glancing toward the door with the hole in it, he brightened. *Hey, at least they were smart enough to make something to protect us from the beam.* He regarded the barrier with satisfaction; nine half inch metal plates, alternating lead, steel, and titanium, stood propped up between the mouth of the cave, the source of the deadly microwave beam that had killed several people over the course of the last few centuries (the last one just a few months ago had been one of their comrades), and the hidden door leading to this chamber. A door now bearing a small hole; mute evidence of the event that had cost a man his life. The large dish antenna set just outside the cave mouth and slightly to one side was in amazingly good condition considering the length of time it had been there, having apparently been coated in some kind of preservative.

"These bigger rocks are going to be a problem. They must weigh as much as two grown men," one of them said unhappily as he carefully put the last of the smaller rocks in the pile now dominating the center of the room. *Thank goodness all the stuff on the other side is still okay,* he mused.

The other man mopped his face with a cloth pulled from his pocket. "Yeah, I know Sam. I thought of that yesterday, and I have the answer." He picked up the leather bag that had drawn several curious looks when they climbed the stairs to get here, and pulled out a hammer and chisel. "All we have to do is break them up into two or three pieces, and that should take care of it." Walking over next to his friend, he pointed. "See that one there? It's got a crack right smack dab in the middle, or pretty close. I bet a few good wacks and that sucker will break right in half!" Settling the goggles over his eyes, and putting on the heavy work gloves, he suited actions to words, and placing the chisel in the crack, raised the hammer. Just as predicted, less than five minutes work, and the stones lay in two nearly equal pieces. A few minutes later, after some grunting and sweating, the two pieces had joined their smaller brethren in the center of the room.

One of the guards cleared his throat. "We have to go down and check the tunnel. Just don't open the outer door and you'll be fine."

Sam nodded in agreement, scowling slightly. He said to himself, *you guys are lucky. The last group already cleared the rocks away from the door, the outer corridor and that whole area at the top of the stairs.* He then picked up his canteen, opened it, and handed it to his companion with a flourish. "The man who solves the problem drinks first. All hail Max slayer of big rocks!"

Taking off his goggles, Max made a sweeping bow and gravely accepted the canteen. "Why thank you, my good man. It was no trouble, no trouble at all." He drank deeply, then handed it back so his companion could follow suit. Refreshed, the two returned to their labors, and within a couple of hours, only one large rock remained. Unfortunately, the top side was flat and smooth. A few minutes of searching for a suitable crevice yielded nothing and several attempts in various places produced nothing but a few small chips, and some barely noticeable scars in the rock. The two backed off to consider.

"Blast it, we're almost done! Do you want to try lifting it?"

"Nah, I almost got a hernia with the bigger piece of that

second one, let alone this monster. Hey Sam, how about we try and knock a few pieces off the sides?"

"Are you kidding? That would take forever! Although..." He paused. "What the heck, maybe it's got cracks on the inside. Let's give it a shot." He picked up the chisel, and, holding it firmly in one hand, placed it about an inch from one side of the rock. "Go ahead."

Max took careful aim and swung the hammer. After several tries a small piece flew off, striking him painfully on the arm. With a curse Sam threw down the chisel, which bounced off the rock into one of the panels. There were several small sparks followed by a wisp of smoke, and behind them on one of the undamaged panels across the room, a large light briefly flared an ominous red before flickering and dying.

The two men looked at each other, then back at the once again quiescent panel. When a full minute had passed with no further activity, Sam reached over, and gingerly picked up the chisel. He backed up several steps, and said softly, "Did you see that?"

The answer came quietly, but forcely. "No, and neither did you!"

His companion nodded slowly. "I think we're done for the day. We'll have to come back with some levers or something."

They hurriedly picked up their gear, and with a last backward glance, walked through the door and past the two bored men standing guard. "We...uh...have to rig up something to move a large rock. We'll be back tomorrow...hopefully."

The guards nodded. One of them yawned and the two workmen headed down the tunnel toward the stairs.

Thousands of miles overhead, in a control room that had been abandoned for centuries, a circuit flared into life and shorted, briefly glowing with a blinding light before the ancient wires finally melted through. The now unconnected piece of wire floated until it landed across several other heavily corroded wires, resulting in large showers of sparks. Several messages appeared briefly on the displays scattered about the room.

FIRE IN ENGINEERING... CONTROL SYSTEM 37A OFFLINE... CONTAMINATION WARNING IN HYDROPONICS TANK 7... HULL BREACH IN SECTION 274C... SHUTTLE LAUNCH FAILURE... ACTIVATING EMERGENCY BEACON IN 5...4...3...2...1. Across the room an ancient machine stirred into reluctant life and another message to the dead flashed across a display. EMERGENCY BEACON ACTIVATED. The ancient Bernholtz transmitter began its lonely work. A required piece of hardware on all spacecraft, the Bernholtz transmitter was reserved solely for emergencies. Although the miraculous machine allowed nearly instantaneous communication across light years of empty space, like the Ultra Low Frequency radios of Earth, its bandwidth was so low that it took several minutes to transmit a single character. Several days passed as the patient machine sent its required message, the universally agreed upon symbol for 'HELP' followed by an ID then the galactic coordinates of the source. Finished, it began again, and again. The ancient machine would continue its duty until it was reset, destroyed or ran out of power. This particular unit was hooked directly into the Casimir generators. Drawing upon an anomaly in space-time, these devices had continued to produce power for over 1,000 years, and most likely would continue to do so for another thousand.

~つC~

ACROSS THE GALAXY, BERNHOLTZ RECEIVERS WERE activating. Most, not recognizing the location or the identification code, would either file it under interesting phenomena or simply ignore it.

~つC~

ROUGHLY 150 LIGHT YEARS AWAY, ALOD-BOI-GAZAREE clicked his left pincer sharply in the "alert" pattern to summon his superior, while four of his lesser grippers adjusted the controls of the device that had just supplied the direction, and would eventually determine the distance of the emergency signal detected during the previous day cycle. While the Klackari confederation had never bothered to decipher the messages that followed, they DID know the sequence that translated as HELP, and where someone needed help, there were frequently spoils to be had, and sometimes even slaves to be sold.

Alod-ben-grsch scuttled into the room, his eight feet making a soft swishing sound on the hard surface, mandibles grinding out the command to report. "What is it, Gazaree?" Extending his legs as far as possible, he rose to his full height of 29" in order to aim his central eye at the console.

Gazaree, crouched in the fluid bath necessary to keep his body hydrated during his six hour shift, responded respectfully, "The target direction has been calculated." He waved one of his greater grippers at the figures glowing on the screen. "I can now say it is closer than 50 kavar, and the distance should be available by the end of shift, or soon after."

"Ah, excellent." Grsch left the room to give the new course to the bridge crew. After that, he proceeded to the records room to begin his research on what targets might lie in that direction. Thus far they only knew that it was less than 50 kavar away. He reached for a map case with his pincers, and spread it flat with both of his greater grippers. One of the lesser grippers that were tracing possible paths in the right direction had just settled on a system listed as "anomalous-unexplored", when a few of the facets of his left eye detected movement nearby. Turning to face it, he saw Alod-bar-gaz, the ship's first officer. He quickly snapped both pincers shut and touched them to his mandibles in a sharp salute.

Gaz's mandibles clicked rapidly as he chuckled, "It's okay Grsch, there's no one else here, so I'm just your cousin Gaz." Waving a greater gripper at the map, he went on. "Any luck? I heard the order to change course."

"Well, we don't have a good distance yet, but I found something about 25 kavar away in the right direction that bears looking at." Spreading the map again, he indicated the system in question. "This one. It's listed as anomalous.

Apparently, there's something about it that restricts normal travel, so I'm thinking maybe some nice, fat, slow colony ship got itself in trouble."

"Hmmm, yes, I see. Slaves are a pain. You have to feed them, guard them, and sometimes listen to all kinds of garbage talk, but if you get lucky they can be worth a fortune. For example, because of the construction of those mining shafts on Jharta 5, there is a big spike in the market for tall slaves with strong manipulators. If we could glom onto a whole shipful of those, we'll be sitting pretty for a long time. Keep looking, and I'll update the captain."

~ɔC~

Mish349 of the Minthar Collective waited patiently as the message came through with what most races considered agonizing slowness. There was a high pitched squeal from one of the speakers. Rearing up slightly on his hind legs, he reached out with his right tentacle, and carefully adjusted the gain. Unlike the vast majority of his race, Mish349 could tolerate being in an enclosed space for long periods of time. He had already passed through two meditation cycles, and was about to enter a third when the station communicator signaled for attention. "Mish349...."

"Signal?" The Minthar, being partially telepathic among themselves as well as being empathic with most others, were noted for not wasting words.

"In progress...Direction...95%, Distance soon, translation pending."

"Classification?"

"Emergency beacon - 97.5%."

"Response vessel readied. Inform at direction 98%...remain well." This last was accompanied by a burst of warmth and appreciation.

"Noted." He sent back the telepathic equivalent of a smile. The communicator went silent. Elsewhere on the giant station a starship sat ready, waiting for the information that would send it on its way. The Mithar were cautious to a fault. To them,sending a vessel with a direction certainty of *only* 98% was considered somewhat hasty, but this appeared to be an emergency. Being empaths, the troubles of others actually WERE painful to them, and they had long since taken to helping anyone in trouble.

MIsh349 pranced a little in place to ease sore muscles. Feeling hungry, he reached into the bin next to his workstation and extracted a tilp root. He ate quickly, breaking the root into several smaller pieces with a couple of quick snaps of his beak. Shortly thereafter, he began to feel the urge to gallop and prepared once again to enter his meditation state, reminding his body to become alert at any warning tone from the equipment he was monitoring.

~つC~

SCOTT AND MORGAN WERE SITTING IN THE STUDY DISCUSSING his new "radio" idea when there was a knock at the door. Shortly thereafter a young man entered the room and handed a sealed note to Morgan. After opening and reading it, Morgan growled, and tossed the note on the table next to him. "Lucky you. We have both been invited to attend a gala next week. Some sort of mumbo-jumbo about honoring important people. Phhht."

Scott was puzzled. "That sounds like quite an honor?"

"Not really. My brother just wants to show off that he knows you and introduce you to his circle of fancy friends."

"Brother? I didn't even know you had a brother."

Morgan shrugged. "He's not around very much."

"Should I ask why not?"

Another shrug. "We just move in different circles, have different skills, and different motivations."

When Scott remained silent, Morgan looked at him and sighed. "You see, my older brother Harold is a handsome, well respected member of the diplomatic corps. He has little time for mundane things like running a vineyard, or managing a household. He and most of my family have no respect at all for what I am and what I do. They were about to disown me for taking after my grandfather and learning magic." He smiled slightly. "Right up until my brother made it clear that he had no interest in running the vineyard or maintaining the family home. He and his wife Babbett live in one of those big fancy houses over where the rich people live. You know the type I mean."

Scott snorted. "Yeah, I do. One of the reasons my wife moved to California was to get away from that lifestyle." He frowned. "Her mother is kind of like that and she's really into that New Age stuff, in some ways even more than Lisa."

Morgan looked puzzled. "New Age stuff?"

"Oh, sorry, things like psychics, mind reading, astrology. That kind of thing."

"What's astrology?"

"Some people think the positions of the stars and planets have an effect on their personalities and daily lives. Like, they might say, 'this planet is appearing next to those three stars this month, so I should avoid meeting new people right now'. Or 'my birth sign is XX and yours is YY so we must be incompatible.'" Scott shrugged. "It never made any sense to me, but some people let it control their lives." He went on hastily, "Lisa and her mom aren't that bad but they kind of buy into it somewhat."

Morgan shrugged as well. "Well, at least my brother isn't into that kind of thing, although I think Babette may be, at least a little. It sounds like something she would buy into."

CHAPTER
Three

TO SAY THAT LISA HATHAWAY WAS DEPRESSED THAT DAY WAS putting it mildly. The horror of Scott's death in the freak explosion that destroyed the power station had been bad enough, but when they couldn't find ANY trace of her husband, it had become almost too much to bear.

"I...I never even got to bury him," she sobbed, sitting slumped in the chair in her therapist's office. "At...at least B...Becky Higgins had something to bury. I have nothing." She buried her face in her hands.

"I realize how bad that must feel," Dr. Thomas Johnson said sympathetically, reaching across the desk and handing her a tissue. "Lack of closure can make a bad situation even worse." He let her cry for a moment, then asked gently, "How about your work? We both felt that getting back to running the yoga studio would be good for you."

Lisa brightened somewhat. "Oh...VERY well, everyone has been understanding, and they are all willing to pitch in so I only have to go in when the children are in school. And there is never an issue when I need to take personal time. Even when I do the scheduling from home, it helps me feel…I don't know…useful? Connected?"

He smiled. "I'm so glad. And how are the children holding up?" He quickly glanced at the notes in front of him. "Are Gwen and Danny seeing a grief counselor? At school perhaps?" Another glance. "I know John Seymore and he is really good with children."

Lisa looked up, eyes red. "Yes, they both say he's nice, but poor Gwennie really misses her daddy. They were very close. Danny has been very supportive but I know he isn't sleeping well, I can hear him walking around…" she trailed off guiltily.

"Lisa, I thought you said you were sleeping through the night?" He looked at his notepad again and frowned. "Aren't those pills working? I can give you something else…."

"No, no. I told you I don't want to be drugged asleep! What if Scott wants to talk to me?"

Dr. Johnson surreptitiously made a note on his pad. "Lisa…we talked about this. Scott is gone…he can't talk to you."

"But, what about all the little things that moved in my purse? My lipstick, my mascara, my lip gloss, they moved from the makeup case into the side pocket! I ALWAYS keep them together in the makeup case. Why would they be in the side pocket? And my locket with Scott's picture. It was in my bureau inside the jewelry box, then one day it was outside the box. And, and my car keys, what about my car keys? You KNOW I never ever put them anywhere but in the special bowl on the counter, but yet one day there they were on the floor! And how about the time..." The words seemed to be coming faster and faster.

"Lisa, we've talked about all these things. You know..."

"But Doctor, you remember how my great grandma used to send me messages after she passed! What about the...the nightmares? Why would I suddenly have night-mares about...you know...THAT night? The night that I was...well, the night my Scottie rescued me? Only now he isn't there, and those men are going to hurt me! I haven't dreamed about that in years, you know I haven't...And what about –"

"Lisa, please! We talked about all these things. With Scott gone it's only natural that your mind dwells on when you fell in love, and your mind is playing tricks on you by making you forget where you put things. We've talked about all of this."

"REALLY! Well, NOW my wedding ring is missing. It's gone, completely gone! I never, EVER put that ring anywhere but in my jewelry box or on my finger. Never. Now it's...it's gone, vanished! All these things, everything that's moved, they're things my husband touched, EVERY-THING!" Tears were flowing freely and she began to tremble.

"Lisa, listen to me! It's very important –" There was a soft chime from the clock on the desk. The doctor sighed. "I'm afraid our time is up. Look, I'm prescribing you a mild sedative to use during the day, and I urge you to take a sleeping pill at least every other day." He wrote on a pad taken from his desk drawer, tore off, and handed her the paper on top. She took it with visible reluctance, nodded slowly, and rose to leave. "Lisa?" She turned back to face him. "Why don't you leave through the side exit, and then rest in the lobby for a little while until you feel a bit better." She straightened her shoulders, and turned to leave through a different door on the other side of the room. "I'll see you next week."

Lisa spent about 20 minutes in the lobby of the building pretending to read a magazine before stopping in the ladies room to repair her makeup. Opening her makeup case, she saw that now the tweezers were in the compartment with her credit cards, and smiling sadly, she said softly, "Thank you Scott, I know you're watching." Looking around to make sure she was alone, she went on. "I guess I have to take these pills or the doctor will be upset with me." Then she brightened slightly. "But I won't take them on Fridays or Saturdays in case you want to talk to me darling."

Driving very carefully, she dutifully dropped off the new prescription at the pharmacy before returning to work. She was greeted with smiles.

"Hey, boss!"

"Welcome back, Mrs. H. Good to see you."

"Hi Lisa, Mrs. Franks called and wanted to reschedule. I offered to take care of her myself, but she insisted on you. She said you always seem to know how she's feeling, and she just loves talking to you."

Lisa laughed. "She's nice. I like her, but she does get kind of depressed sometimes since her husband left her.

I'm just lucky enough to make her feel better. I can certainly understand her being lonely because of...you know." There were several knowing nods. She asked, "Do I need to call her?"

"Yes. I took a look at your schedule and tentatively booked her for next Thursday from 2:00 to 3:00. You just have to call to confirm."

"Thursday...Thursday...." Lisa frowned briefly, then her face cleared. "Oh, sure. That should be fine. I'll go call her. Did she say if she was going to be around this afternoon, or should I try her tonight?"

"She said she had laundry to do and should be there all afternoon."

Nodding, Lisa headed for her office. "Okay, I'll go call her now. Thanks a lot for taking care of that."

"No problem."

The remainder of the afternoon at the studio went smoothly.

Stopping at the grocery store on her way home, she forced herself to smile pleasantly as she pushed the cart up and down the aisles. Even after over a year, everything still reminded her of Scott. The smell of fresh bread in the pastry section reminded her that he wouldn't be there for breakfast. The sight of his favorite tomato sauce reminded her he wouldn't be there for dinner, although she did decide to make his favorite meatloaf since both of the children liked it as well. She quickly purchased the rest of the ingredients and left.

Arriving home after a quick stop at the pharmacy to pick up the now ready prescription, she carefully parked in the garage, and took her bags into the house. She dutifully took one of the new pills, and feeling a little better, began to fix the meatloaf. By the time it was nearly baked, the sound of the school bus announced the arrival of her children, Danny and Gwen. Shortly thereafter she heard the sound of youthful voices bickering and the slamming of the front door. There was a brief silence followed by a young male voice exclaiming excitedly, "Hey! Do I smell meatloaf? Yum, thanks Mom!"

Lisa's spirits lifted as she quickly hugged her children. "Well, you asked for it, and since you both have been good about homework all week, I thought it would be a good time for it. Oh, and Gwen, we will be having tapioca for dessert." She was rewarded by a pair of happy smiles. The children quickly did their homework, and the three of them sat down to a congenial family dinner, and a quiet evening of TV. The children went to bed, and a calmer, happier Lisa dutifully took her sleep aid, and for once had a full night of restful sleep and awoke refreshed.

The next day, after Danny and Gwen had left for school, Lisa decided to call for an appointment with her favorite psychic. "Hi, Maria? Do you have any free time today? I really need to talk…no that won't work. I want to be here when the kids get home from school. Yes, I know they are old enough, but…no, sorry I guess today won't work. Tomorrow morning? Yes, of course, ten o'clock will be fine. Yes, I'll remember…donuts and coffee? Yes. of course. You like the raspberry, right? Great, I'll see you then. Bye, bye."

On the following morning, Lisa eagerly left, went to the

drive through of the local Donut Delight and, after parking in the back of a small building, took the elevator to the third floor.

Reaching the door labeled "Madam Maria...Personal Readings", she opened the door and entered, smiling at the little chiming sound that announced her entry. A slightly heavyset woman in her forties wearing a colorful shawl entered from the back. "Well, hello Lisa! How are you feeling today?" She closed her eyes and extended her hands over Lisa's head for a moment before continuing, "Oh dear, your aura looks troubled. Would you like to come and take a seat in the back?"

"Yes please. Oh," holding out a cup and a small bag, "...cream with two sugars, and a raspberry filled donut."

"Why thank you, my dear, that was so thoughtful of you." The two women walked through a door and the beaded curtain behind it into a small, dimly lit room, sporting a small table covered with an ornate table cloth embroidered with astrological signs. There was a pack of tarot cards and a large, round ball of clear glass in the center, supported by what appeared to be a gold frame. "Please be seated," the woman intoned in a slightly altered voice, vaguely gesturing at a small gilt box next to the tarot cards.

Lisa sat down. "Oh, of course." She reached into her purse and placed several bills in the box. "I'm sorry to bother you, but I really miss my husband and you are so easy to talk to."

Maria smiled, her eyes flickering briefly toward the box. "It's no problem, really. I am always here for you."

She reached across the table. "Here, take my hand and let's see if we can get a connection."

A short while later the woman sighed. "I am so sorry sweetie. I can almost feel his presence, but sometimes the veil is too heavy." She frowned. "I do get feelings that perhaps the children are troubled...Danny especially?"

Lisa sighed. "It's been hard on both of them, but, well, it had been planned that Danny would go back East to M.I.T. That way, not only could he get a great education, but he would be near my parents too. Now he has been talking about going to a local college so we can stay together as a family. My parents are saying that they REALLY want him to come. I...I'm not sure which would be better."

"You should talk about it as a family, and don't forget to include Gwen as well. This will affect her too."

"I will, and thank you."

"Certainly, do you want to come back tomorrow and we could try again?"

Lisa frowned. "I'm not sure...the next check from that insurance annuity doesn't come in till Friday. Could I come back on Monday or Tuesday?"

"Why certainly my dear, but don't wait too long. We don't want the connection to fade."

That evening Lisa and Danny had a brief discussion regarding college. They discussed the original plan for Danny to go to M.I.T. while living with Lisa's parents in nearby Wellesley. The whole family had been onboard with this, and the grandparents had eagerly planned on redecorating one of their spare bedrooms. Danny now wanted to stay in California and go to a local college. Neither of them really wanted to back down and nothing was resolved. Gwen stated glumly that she didn't really care either way.

Several days later Danny laid a pamphlet on the table as they were finishing supper. "Mom, I think I found a way to do what we both want. I talked to my guidance counselor and called the admissions office at M.I.T. It turns out that M.I.T. has an arrangement with one of the local community colleges that if you agree to take a certain set of courses and maintain at least a 3.0 average, you will be guaranteed a spot in the engineering program, and all courses that you get an A or B in will transfer with full credit. That way I can stay here another two years and still go live with Grandma and Grandpa and get a degree from M.I.T. What do you think?"

Lisa felt a burst of pride. "Well, first, I think you acted very maturely, and no matter what we decide, I am proud of you." She picked up the brochure. "Let me look at this and talk it over with your grandparents. But, I think this might work. What do you think, Gwen?"

Gwen shrugged and said dully, "That sounds okay."

OVER THE NEXT FEW DAYS LISA CONSIDERED DANNY'S IDEA. *I really would miss him terribly, especially now, and I know Gwen would too, although she won't admit it. Maybe this would be for the best.*

After an extended phone call with her parents, who,

although admitted to being somewhat disappointed, also thought this might be for the best, she again sat down to talk with her son and daughter. "Danny, Gwen, I thought this over and talked to your grandparents and we agreed that this is a reasonable compromise." She smiled happily. "Go ahead and make your plans. Let me know if you need any help with forms or anything."

Danny smiled back. "Thanks Mom, and thank Grandma and Grandpa for understanding. I can take care of this myself, I think. You may have to sign a few things though." Turning to his sister, "How about you Gwennie? Are you okay with this?"

Gwen smiled, "Well, I WAS looking forward to not having you around to bug me, but I guess that will have to wait." Perking up a little, she continued, "Hey Mom, I got a text message from the stable today. They had a riding group cancel on them and they'll have free horses this Saturday. Could we go riding...please?"

Lisa considered it briefly. *Gwennie REALLY loves horses...this would be good for her!* "That does sound good. Tell them we can come about one o'clock. Would you like to come too, Danny?"

Her son shrugged. "Yeah, I guess so. I have plans to watch a video with Charlie, but that's not until nine or so." He smirked. "I can help keep an eye on Gwennie so she doesn't wander off and get lost again."

"That happened ONCE, you dweeb! And I was ten! Let it go or lose some teeth!"

"GWENDOLYN! Do NOT threaten your brother! Danny, would you care to reconsider your statement?"

Danny tried to hide a smile. "Yeah, yeah. I'm sorry for implying that you might get lost...again."

"Children please! What would your fa..." Lisa's voice trailed off, and her face crumpled.

Gwen quickly rose and put her arm around her mother. "Look what you did! Happy now?"

Danny looked stricken. "I'm sorry, Mom. Geez, I was just kidding around." He also rose to embrace his mother.

Lisa sniffled. "That's okay kids. I'll be okay." She sniffed loudly. "I think supper is almost ready. Danny, please set the table while Gwen checks on the chicken. I'll be there in a minute."

CHAPTER
Four

Scott carefully smoothed down the red tunic that now announced his new status as a Journeyman magician. *Good Lord, am I glad that's over. I know it didn't really last all day but it sure felt like it!* Waving to the throng of spectators, he took his leave. Morgan had warned him that magician promotions were typically (or generally) poorly attended, but because it was for the "great hero, Scott," it might draw a crowd. It did. His guards, lurking carefully on the sidelines, eyes scanning the crowd, had been clearly displeased, but the smiling presence of Count Wesley and the famous caravan master Armis had calmed them somewhat. Now it was finally over. *I can't wait to see if my 'magic radio' idea works!*

Morgan said slowly, "So let me make sure I understand." He indicated the collection of items on the table in front of them. "You want these two crystals set up so that when one of them vibrates, the other one does too?"

Receiving a nod, he went on, "Then if the crystal is made to vibrate from the outside, you want it to make the...what did you call it? Talker?"

"Speaker."

"Okay, speaker. You want that to vibrate, but much slower, so that it makes a sound we can hear." Another nod. "But then you also want it to work in reverse, so, if someone talks into the speaker it makes the crystal vibrate and activates the other one." He sighed, then frowned. "Now you said you thought the two devices might have to be able to...ah...see each other for this to work?"

"I've been thinking about that and I'm pretty sure that if there is something to...um...bounce the signal off of...that might work too."

Morgan's eyebrows furrowed. "I don't follow."

"Well suppose one of them was on the city wall, and the other was several mils up the valley. They can't see each other, but both can see the top of the keep. So if you put, say, a big shield on a pole, then the signal could bounce off that."

Morgan looked thoughtful. "I think I see." He suddenly scowled. "Wait, how in the world could we use this to talk to Landbelow if there has to be something in the middle that both can see? What are we supposed to do, build a tower a hundred mils high to bounce the signal off of? There's no way we can put something in the middle that both can see!" His face got a look of horror. "You aren't going to tell me we have to build towers every few mils, I hope."

Scott smiled. "Why, no. I thought we would use things that are already there."

Morgan looked more puzzled than ever. "The mountains aren't high enough, if that's what you were thinking. And there's nothing else of significance in between...." He paused, sighing heavily. "I know that look. What shocking revelation do you have for me now?"

Scott pointed up. "I was thinking of the moons."

Morgan turned pale, and his mouth dropped open. "Are you serious? What kind of power do you think we can put out to be able to bounce a...signal...off one of the moons! Do you have any idea how far away they are?"

"It would probably take a lot less power than you might think. Just as an example, Those weapons Geon's people use could easily bounce light off one of the moons and back."

Morgan's eyebrows shot up, and he smiled slightly. "Is THAT why you were so anxious to be able to feed them?"

"No, oddly enough it never really occurred to me." He thought for a moment. "It would probably be just as hard to interface those with a magic item as it would be to do it from scratch."

Morgan picked up the two crystals and regarded them thoughtfully. "Well, why don't we get started."

It took the better part of three days before tapping one of the crystals caused the other to make the same sound. It was while they were congratulating each other that a somewhat dusty Brandon knocked on the door. "Hi, the caravan made good time on the way back, so I'm here a day early. What's new?" Morgan opened the door for him, and his mouth dropped open and his eyes widened in shock. He slowly began to smile. "Well, hello Journeyman Scott!" With a quizzical look at Morgan he went on, "I didn't realize I was gone that long."

Morgan snapped "Are you questioning me, boy?" Before laughing and saying, "Unfortunately Scott here is temperamentally unsuited to be either a Student or an Apprentice, so it was either this, or we might have killed each other." He sobered. "In all honesty, his skill at meditation is superior to some Elites I could mention, and his control is quite good as well." He smiled broadly. "You are just in time to witness the newest breakthrough in communications...Scott," gesturing at the worktable, "Go ahead and show him.

Grinning happily, Scott picked up a small hammer and dramatically tapped one of the crystals. The slightly musical tone was echoed by an identical tone from across the room. Brandon looked at the crystal and hammer, looked at Scott and Morgan, both smiling, and said slowly, "I don't get it."

Morgan chuckled. "Why don't you show him again. Watch and listen carefully, my young friend."

Scott repeated the operation while Brandon watched carefully. "I...uh...still don't get it. Is something supposed to happen?"

Scott chuckled, "Go listen carefully to that one," he said, pointing across the room. Brandon obediently walked across the room and stood next to the other crystal. This time, when the crystal next to him made a sound in response to the other one being tapped, he said slowly, "Uh...okay, I hear it, but I don't get the significance."

Scott said carefully, "The significance is that the two crystals are...tied together so that when one vibrates, so does the other one. If this works the way we hope, then it won't matter how far apart they are."

Brandon's eyes widened. He said excitedly, "You mean like your telephone things, only from farther away?"

"Yes, exactly. They may need line-of-sight, but if so I think we can bounce the signal off one of the moons."

Brandon blinked. "Bounce a...signal?...Off one of the moons? So it would only work part of the time?"

Scott shrugged. "Yeah, It might. But for places really far apart, you need something high enough so both places can see it at the same time." He held up his hand as Brandon started to speak. "And the mountains aren't high enough either."

Brandon smiled. "I was going to say why not use the ancient spaceship. It's always in the same place. Or is it not big enough?" Then he looked embarrassed. "Oh, it's too far away, right?"

Scott's mouth dropped open. He said in a quiet voice, "Uh...no it is neither too small nor too far away. I just didn't think of it. It might be a little hard to get the direction exactly right, but other than that it should work." He bowed, pretending to doff a non-existent hat. "Once again, you've come up with something important that I overlooked. My hat is off to you."

Brandon looked pleased and puzzled at the same time. "Your hat is...never mind. You are most welcome." He also made a sweeping bow, and both of them laughed until they were interrupted by a slightly grumpy voice. "That's very amusing, but we do have work to do."

Scott caught Brandon's eye, and they both knelt and said loudly, "YES MASTER."

Morgan sighed and rolled his eyes. "If you are both quite finished...."

Several days later, Brandon carried one of the pair of devices they had created to a spot on the city wall while Scott carried the other to the far end of the city. Looking around to make sure he was alone except for his guards, he pointed the narrow end of the device at the tiny figure in the distance, and clearing his throat, said, "Brandon can you hear me?" Getting no response, he repeated it several more times before glumly walking back to Morgan's home, only to see Brandon waiting for him with a quizzical smile on his face. "Scott, I could hear you just fine, but I guess you couldn't hear me?"

Scott said in surprise, "You could hear me? I didn't hear a thing." He ran his hands through his hair. "I don't understand. It worked fine in the lab."

Brandon said thoughtfully, "Didn't you say that these things have the 'telephone' as part of them? Maybe they were so close in the lab that THOSE were working. Is that possible?"

Scott grimaced, "I wouldn't have thought so, but that does make sense." He brightened. "You said you could hear me?" He got an enthusiastic nod in response. "So it works one way, at least. Worse comes to worst, we'll have to use them in pairs." They had reached the lab by now, and found Morgan waiting for them.

"I heard your voices in the hall. How did it go?"

Scott sighed. "Well, they work, but only in one direction. I think we should test the range and line-of-sight issues next. What do you think?"

Morgan said, "I mostly agree. First, we should make another pair, otherwise they will be very difficult to test across any real distance." He gestured curtly toward the lab door. "Work first, play later."

Now that they knew exactly what they were doing, it took them only a few hours to make the second pair. Morgan grunted with satisfaction. Glancing out the window at the sun low on the horizon, he said, "I think we've done enough for one day..." silencing Brandon with a look, "Yes, yes, I know. You want to run right out and test it now, but it will be dark soon. So we're going to eat, plan exactly what to do, and start fresh tomorrow. Okay...OKAY!" He snapped, as Brandon and Scott both started to speak.

They were interrupted by a knock on the door. At a gesture from Morgan, Brandon went over and opened it. "Hello...oh hi. Yeah sure...say hi to your wife for me." He closed the door.

"That was Fredo, he said to tell you his brother-in-law is feeling a little better since you sent the potions. What's he talking about?"

Morgan snorted. "He seems to think magic is the answer to everything, so I mixed some medicinal herbs in brandy and told him it was a healing potion." He chuckled, "I'm glad it seemed to help." Brandon and Scott both seemed to develop coughing fits at hearing this.

Shortly, they both subsided, and dutifully followed Morgan to his dining chamber. After discussing the next day at length, they all went to bed.

The next day was overcast and cold. Morgan suggested waiting for better weather, but Scott and Brandon were both too eager to get started. Each of them took two of the devices and slogged to their previous positions, accompanied by their wet and very unhappy guards.

Scott had tied the two devices loosely together, having told Brandon it meant basically only having to aim one thing instead of two. One of his guards, a burly fellow named Karg, who had a shock of unruly black hair and an engaging smile, said quietly, "If ye don't mind me askin', what are these things sposed to be good fur?"

Scott smiled, "We hope they'll let people talk back and forth over really long distances."

John, his other guard, had stepped closer as well. "You mean like from the castle to the center of town?"

"No, like from here to the capital, or even farther."

The two regarded him with awe. After exchanging glances, John said diffidently, "I suppose it isn't any of my business, but how is it that you come up with all these new ideas so quick? I mean, I've been talking to mages off and on most of my life, and some of them are pretty smart, but...."

Scott shrugged. "Well, I've read an awful lot, and talked to a lot of different people with different ideas, but mostly I guess I just think differently than most people."

After thinking about it for a couple of minutes, John said, "Well, whatever the reason we are all glad that you're here...Ah...here we are." He gestured toward the wall visible in the distance.

Scott quickly aimed his device at the wall, smiling as he steadied it on the special support painstakingly developed just for this purpose, a forked stick. He smiled inwardly at the look on Brandon's face when he had displayed his 'specialized communicator support structure'. Squinting along the edge as he adjusted the angle, he realized that he should add a telescope to help with aiming. Taking a deep breath, he activated the device and said slowly and distinctly, "Brandon can you hear me?" As he waited for a reply, he heard a faint noise somewhat like a small dog growling. After several seconds had gone by, he repeated the call, and was answered!

"Yes, I can hear you! You sound funny, though."

The words were overlaid by a louder version of the growling noise. After a short conversation, he regarded the pair of devices thoughtfully, and carefully untying them, he asked one of his guards to hold one. The growling lessened. At a gesture the guard slowly moved the other device until it was about two feet away. The growling grew fainter and finally stopped altogether. He called out, "Brandon, let's head back. There are a couple more issues to fix."

After days of tedious experimentation, they found that a thin lead plate between the two parts of the device was enough to stop what Scott was sure was feedback. *Just like the squeal when you hold a microphone too close to a speaker.* He grumbled to himself. *I should have thought of that.* They took an extra day to fasten a small telescope to each device, and then waited three more days for a carpenter and a couple of metalsmiths to create a better support for what was becoming a somewhat cumbersome setup. Their new support consisted of clamps, swivels and tightening knobs mounted on a tripod. Lifting the communicator and telescope, Scott estimated that it weighed somewhere around 20-25 pounds, with the tripod adding another 10 or so. He sighed. *I guess now we'll have to design some kind of carrying case.* Stepping back, he almost laughed at its appearance. Each communicator was a tube about 3 inches in diameter and about 2 feet long. Two of them had been fastened together with the thin plate between them, and a wooden stock to help with aiming. To speed things up, they had used the stock from a crossbow, making the whole thing resemble an enormous double barrelled shotgun. Added to that was a two foot long telescope about a foot in diameter mounted on top.

After the first completely successful test from the city to the wall, more testing over the following two weeks showed that the devices did indeed have to "see each other" in order to work. Morgan was pleased with the results so far. The last test had been from the top of the great keep to a spot on a mountaintop more than three days' travel away. Scott had privately estimated the distance to be around 50 miles or so. The results had also shown that the aiming was not as critical as they had first feared. The test conversations had continued until the aim had been at a point over a mile from the target, albeit somewhat weak and fuzzy. A test from the city wall to the far side of the castle via a metal shield was strikingly successful, it being discovered that almost any solid object would work, although metal seemed best. The aiming was more important for this, although not as critical as they had first thought.

Scott smiled happily as they discussed the results over dinner. "It seems that the beam is not as tight as I thought it would be." *And to think Morgan thought I was wasting my time designing a protractor.* He had been able to determine that the beam was about 2 or 3 degrees wide. Fortunately, the Enimnorians were familiar with trigonometry, and they could calculate that the spread at 50 miles was over a mile and a half, and it would be about 700 miles across when it reached the ancient asteroid ship. *Well, maybe the telescope was a bit of overkill,* he thought ruefully. *A simple tube with crosshairs might be good enough. I'll have to remember to discuss it with Morgan before we build any more of these.*

Now came the moment of truth. Brandon set off with a small party of soldiers to set up on the opposite side of the pass through the mountains. First they would try bouncing the signal off the inner moon. One of Morgan's friends had carefully worked out a schedule of when it would be in the best position. Then if that worked, they would try using the asteroid ship, Morgan's friend having shown them how to find it in the night sky.

A week later, the party made camp and prepared for the first test. Since Morgan's friend had told them that the inner moon would be moving about 30 degrees per mark, which worked out to a little more than one degree in about two minutes, someone would need to keep shifting the device constantly but very slowly. They set up the system on its tripod and got ready.

It had been agreed that they would start one mark after sunset on the eighth day and continue trying for two marks. They would continue this for five nights, or until they got an answer. Depending on what happened they would then either leave or continue with the next part of the test. At the agreed upon time, Brandon cleared his throat, and said loudly and slowly, "We're here. Can anyone hear me? Hello, can anyone hear me?" He kept this up for several minutes while those around him fidgeted quietly. Finally, a voice responded.

"Yes! We can hear you. It's faint but we can hear you!" The sound was faint and distorted, as though the speaker had a sore throat. They exchanged pleasantries for a short while, then agreed to try using the asteroid ship in exactly one mark. This was actually somewhat easier, since the ship remained forever stationary in the sky. It only took a short while to locate it and set up, then a dozen anxious faces watched the timing candle slowly burn down.

Finally, Brandon began speaking again. After almost a mark he cast the enhanced hearing spell and tried again. This time he thought he could hear a faint voice repeating, "Hello, can you hear me? Hello? Hello, can you hear me?" But he was not absolutely certain. After two more marks the exhausted and disappointed group went to bed.

They tried again the following night and the night after that. Finally, after the agreed upon five days, the group packed and returned home.

That same fifth day saw a somewhat dejected and annoyed Scott speaking to an angry Morgan. "Scott, I don't see why you are so upset. It WORKED! What part of that is so hard to understand? I don't see any reason to waste more time and more crystals just because it didn't work exactly like you wanted it to." Morgan had been pacing back and forth. Finally, he sat down. "So that's that!"

Scott jumped to his feet. "No, it isn't!" He almost snarled. "It DIDN'T really work. We could barely hear each other and this is a lot closer than Dener Peak and Landbelow!" I want to establish RELIABLE communications, not something that's hit or miss and barely audible!" He took a couple of deep breaths and sat back down. "Please, this could be very important someday. I understand about the crystals, but we will have to hand deliver at least one of these anyway, and hopefully we can find some more crystals at the same time." He hesitated. "I don't know why but my gut is telling me that fast effective communications between us and Landbelow could be absolutely vital someday!"

Morgan suddenly felt a cold chill. *I don't think I've ever seen Scott so passionate about something before!* He bit back a sharp report and regarded his friend thoughtfully. *Maybe he is one of the prescient ones.* "I... you may be right." He sighed and said quietly, "You win. We will try adding another crystal to uh...increase the...strength of the signal." He snorted. "I'm sure Brandon will be just thrilled to be sent out again so soon. I'll let you tell him.

Scott laughed quietly. "Well, fair is fair." He looked at

Morgan. "Maybe I should go this time and spare him the trip."

Morgan said thoughtfully, "Well, I'm sure Brandon would appreciate that but I'm not sure Wesley and Armis would agree." He shrugged. "I'll mention it and see how they react."

Surprisingly, neither Count Wesley nor Armis had a problem with Scott going, although Armis did select some of his best woodsmen and guards to 'keep Scott company' as he put it. So it was that another group set out a mere two days after the return of the first. Scott was pleased that John and Karg were coming along. They had been guarding him for months now and the three of them got along quite well.

"Sir, if you don't mind me askin', why do we have to go so far for this?" John had always been the more inquisitive of the two.

Scott looked at him with a twinkle in his eye and twisted in his saddle, shading his eyes as though searching for someone. Karg snorted and rolled his eyes, while John sighed and rode a little closer and lowered his voice. "Alright, alright...Scott why do we have to go so far?"

"A couple of reasons. First off, we want to get a good angle on the ship, and also, we have to be out of range for anything else so we know for sure whether it's working or not." He hesitated before saying ruefully, "I don't know if you remember or not, but we had trouble before when things worked in the lab, but not across the city?"

"I'm not sure if I realized it at the time, but now that you mention it, yeah I think I do."

"Well, quite a few people are going to a lot of trouble and we REALLY want to be certain everything is okay before we take one of these things all the way to Dener Peak and Landbelow." He smiled. "I'm sure you can imagine Morgan and Wesley's reactions if they mounted an expedition all the way THERE only to have it not work."

John's eyebrows went up. "Huh! Yeah, I can see your point. I don't think I'd want to be anywhere nearby if that happened." He paused briefly, eyes searching the area before returning to Scott. "He said quietly, "You do know that we have to be respectful and call you sir and all that when the others are listening, right?"

Scott said somewhat sourly, "Yeah, I know. 'The amenities must be observed or there will be chaos'," he said as though imitating a teacher at a finishing school. The others laughed, and they rode on in companionable silence.

This time the closer moon was in position by mid afternoon on the appointed day. Squinting into the setting sun, the team carefully set up the tripod and pointed the device at the center of the rising moon.

Scott took a deep breath. "Brandon, are you there? Can you hear me?" After a brief pause, he began again. After only a few minutes, a welcome voice answered clearly, "YES! I can hear you. It's much better than before. This is wonderful. Just give us a half mark and try the other way."

Glancing skyward, Scott replied, "Sorry, there are some clouds in the way, I think we'll have to wait for a while."

By the time the clouds had cleared enough for them to see the stars, it was already dark. After carefully adjusting the direction to point at the ancient spaceship that showed brighter than any other star, Scott once again began sending his hopeful message. After nearly two marks, just when they were about to give up for the night, a voice finally answered. "Hello! Yes we can hear you. Can you hear me?"

Scott's spirits rose considerably. "Yes, Yes! We can hear you just fine. Over."

There was a brief pause. "Over? Over what?"

Scott shuckled to himself. "Sorry, that's what my people say when they are finished talking and it's okay for you to say something. When you are all finished and want to say goodbye, we say 'out'."

Another pause, "Well, okay. Oh, sorry for the delay. Someone was bringing a herd through the pass and we had to move. Um...over."

"I understand. We were starting to get a little worried but this is working just fine! Give my regards to Morgan and we'll try this again at noon tomorrow, just to be sure. Out!"

"Uh...okay...goodbye."

The following noon saw another successful test, and the satisfied group packed up for the journey home. They were met upon their arrival by a smiling Brandon and an uncharacteristically happy Winston.

A very excited Brandon announced, "As soon as we can make another one of these telecoms we're going to go back to Landbelow and deliver it! Then we'll be able to talk to Varney whenever we want. Isn't that great?" Visibly forcing himself to calm down, he gave the amused Scott a significant look and continued, "Maybe we can find some time to do some more exploring too."

Scott smiled back. "Ah, that's why Winston is grinning so broadly!" This earned him a slightly annoyed look. "It HAS been quite a while...you are coming along aren't you?" Receiving a nod in reply he went on, "Wait, what did you call them...", gesturing at the wagon holding the communicator, "...telecoms?"

Brandon flushed slightly. "Well, you call the distance viewer a telescope, so it seemed like a distance communicator should be a telecommunicator, but that seemed too long so...." He looked concerned. "You don't mind that I named it, do you? After all, we had to call them something, and...well...you weren't here," he finished somewhat lamely.

Scott tried to look stern. "Well," he said huffily, "I find that very presumptuous! I, being the inventor, had the right to name them...I was going to call them.." he paused dramatically, "...things-that-let-you talk-to people-who-are far-away', but I suppose it's too late now." He sighed heavily. "I guess 'telecom' will just have to do." Noticing Winston starting to cloud up, he went on more seriously, "Of course it's okay. How soon are we planning on leaving?"

Brandon coughed and said, "Well, we want to make another one of these so we can keep in touch on the way back, and Winston has some stuff he wants to bring."

He nodded to Winston who said gravely, "I have been speaking at length with several of your merchants and we believe we have a list of marketable items. We don't do

much metal working, particularly not just for enjoyment."
He indicated a silvery pendant he was wearing. "I am
certain that things such as this will be well received." He
eyed Brandon. "...And some other things as well..."

Brandon's eyes lit up, and he said excitedly, "You won't
believe it! I know I didn't, but Armis and Morgan talked
the Count into trading some rifles and pistols for one of
their scout weapons...and maybe another..." he hesitated,
"...tester thing that works even better than the one we have
now!"

Scott blinked and said cautiously, "Really? Uh...that
will be great."

CHAPTER
Five

"I don't quite understand. Why don't you think I should go?"

Count Wesley took a deep breath. "Look Scott, you told me yourself that they started to give you the cold shoulder toward the end, right?"

"Well...yes, that IS true, but I...."

"I'm not trying to be offensive here, but I don't know if I really trust these people. Winston is nice enough, but I just have kind of a bad feeling. Now I realize that a magician HAS to go to operate the device, and Brandon is the logical choice since he helped create them, and he's been there before. But I really didn't like having you both gone before, and I just don't see the need this time. I'm sorry."

Scott sighed. "I see your point. I still have a lot to learn, so I guess it's better if I can be near Morgan anyway. Unless of course..."

That got a laugh. "Don't even THINK about suggesting Morgan go! He is far too valuable here."

This time, the expedition had been reduced to less than 60 people (still armed to the teeth) and the trip through the wilderness no longer seemed so arduous. The mood had been lightened considerably by being in daily communication with Enimnori. After the first couple of weeks, they settled on once a week, partly out of a concern by Count Wesley and a few others that the devices might "wear out".

Morgan was a bit irritated at having his ability to talk to Brandon curtailed. "You tell them and tell them, but it never sinks in…If they are going to stop working then they will stop working WHETHER YOU USE THEM OR NOT!" He stopped pacing and scowled. "What the devil are you smiling at?"

His friend and fellow magician Valtir chuckled. "I don't recall your being so upset when they went before and you couldn't talk to them for months. Calm down."

Morgan's face got red, then he sat down and laughed. "You know, you're right. I guess it's just a matter of expectations. Then I COULDN'T talk to them, but now I could if those fools WOULD LET ME!"

～◎◡～

THE CURRENT LEADER OF THE LANDBELOW FACILITY HAD ALSO been feeling somewhat "put upon" lately.

An excerpt from the diary of Martin Dener:

I am beginning to regret choosing Winston as my emissary

to the Enimnori people, oddly enough for the same reason I chose him…he is a close friend and one of the few people I trust absolutely. It has been especially hard with these damaging rumors that have been circulating lately. I know that Franz is behind this, and it was expected, but what is really disturbing is that at least some almost HAD to have come from someone on my staff. I have been able to deal with them up to this point, but it would certainly be easier with Winston here to help me. I know it is wishful thinking, but I have already decided that when he returns I will send Leslie Jons to replace him. I hope the Enimnori people do not have issues with women in positions of authority. I must remember to ask when they return.

～つＣ〜

It seemed to Geon that it had taken far too long, but finally a friendly voice called from behind a screen of scruffy bushes. "Halt and be recognized."

Winston came forward. "Ambassador Zedimore returning. Accompanied by envoys and a trading delegation from Enimnori."

"Advance." A somewhat nervous scout stepped through the bushes and came to attention, ostentatiously pressing the green button on his tocsin before returning it to his belt. "Follow me, sir."

～つＣ〜

It took very little time to show Varney how to set up, aim and activate the "telecom" they were leaving. The negotiations around arranging for a used scout weapon and high quality battery tester took somewhat longer, but once Martin was told that they could have ten rifles AND ten pistols along with several thousand cartridges for both types, his reluctance quickly disappeared.

The selling of the jewelry and other specialty items lasted several days, but finally everyone seemed satisfied and the group packed up to head back. After a brief stop at the peak to have another look at the ancient equipment the group headed back.

Armis trotted his horse over to Brandon's and said quietly, "Any luck?"

Brandon answered happily, "Yes! Very much so. I found quite a few large ones and a big pile of little ones!" He paused before continuing, "I'm pretty sure that micro... whatever Scott spoke of was...uh...active not too long ago. It wouldn't surprise me if there are even more the next time someone comes here."

Armis smiled, nodded, and moved away.

Geon rode over. "Hi. You know, I actually kind of miss having Winston around. Nothing against Leslie, but she seems like more of a...um...." He sat extremely straight and looked around with a scowl on his face. "You know...."

"Yeah, I get the same feeling. I also get the impression she doesn't believe in magic at all." Brandon glanced around and smirked. "She sure has Armis' attention though."

Geon twisted around to 'straighten his saddlebags' before answering. "It sure does look that way, It's kinda hard to tell what she thinks, but I think she MIGHT like him too. Speaking of girls..." He waggled his eyebrows suggestively and pointedly looked ahead at the wagon Marta was driving. "Anything YOU want to talk about?"

"I don't know...well...I'm not sure. I thought she really liked me, but now she seems a bit distant...." his voice trailed off.

"Maybe it's just that Armis has been on her case about it. You know how he is!"

Brandon grunted. "Yeah, I know how he is...'we must ALWAYS be professional on the trail. Leave that nonsense till you get home'...sheesh."

Geon looked thoughtful, "When we get back, why don't you take her to that tavern that has that really nice view of the mountains, or maybe you could pack some food and actually go up there for a romantic getaway."

Brandon brightened. "Hmmm, thanks I may do that." He sat up with a jerk. "Hey, it's a ways off, but I can ask her to the Year End Festival. We could watch the contests together, and we could sit together at the feast and maybe she would dance with me."

~つC~

HIGH ABOVE THE PLANET VARUSHNA, THE KLAKARI SHIP *Finder-of-Spoils* continued in its pole-to-pole orbit, slowly building a rough map of the planet's surface. In the two weeks since their arrival, the ship's occupants had discovered a large inhabited area, and had sent several unmanned probes to begin the population evaluation process.

Somewhat fearfully, Alod-Boi-Gazaree summoned his superior. "Sir, there is still no sign of any life support on that colony ship, and there aren't any communication signals on the planet. We only see animal-powered transportation, and atmospheric soot and contaminants are very low. It appears to be only a level 2 or 3 society..." He hesitated.

"AND...?"

"Uh...they said that the ship has been abandoned for a LONG time and is also VERY unusual..." He paused. "They said that in a way it...isn't really a ship as such, but...."

"Fine...whatever," snarled Alod-ben-grsch, seeing his hopes for any technological plunder dashed. He bounced slightly on his legs to settle his nerves before continuing in a calmer tone. "It could be worse. They could be low-gravity non-builders. Those would hardly be worth the effort of training and shipment."

"Uh, sir...the science crew asked me to tell you that there is something unusual about the moons. They seem too dense."

Grsch snapped both pincers in annoyance. "And I care because...?"

Gazaree tilted his body forward in embarrassment. "They asked me to tell you...."

"Okay, you told me! Are we ready to take some samples yet?"

"Very soon. The collection crew is ready but the flight crew is fixing a minor problem with the shuttle."

"Step it up! We need to know what kind of product we have here so we can contact the right buyers."

"Yes, sir."

~ɔC~

LESS THAN 5,000 MILES AWAY THE MINTHAR SHIP DRIFTED silently and invisibly, having arrived 8 sleep cycles before the Klackaris. Upon detecting their approach, the Minthar had immediately activated the ship's cloaking device, and proceeded to deploy a series of stealthy satellites.

"Back us off, and shift to the opposite side of the planet." The captain had no intention of being discovered in the unlikely event of a cloaking failure. Turning to the science station, she inquired, "EM signal analysis?" The ship's crew had intercepted an intermittent series of electromagnetic signals, some occurring at regular intervals.

"Partly...there seems to be a single pair of strong nodes, as well as regular, weak signals. One of the strong nodes is stationary, while the other is moving away from the area where the weak signals originate."

The captain clicked her beak thoughtfully.

"Language...?"

"There isn't enough for the translator to work yet. Perhaps a couple of more exchanges will do it."

~ɔC~

THE PLANET BELOW HAD ROTATED ON ITS AXIS SEVERAL DOZEN more times before the Minthar ship once again detected a small object separating from the Klackari vessel.

"This may be a slave raid. Is the translator ready yet?"

"We think so. Assuming that what we are receiving is encoded speech then we have enough patterns. We just need to record some spoken words and we should be okay."

~⊃ℭ~

THE GUARDS STATIONED AT THE ENIMNORI GATE TRADED glances and gripped their weapons more tightly as the group of riders approached at a gallop. Among them was a trembling man with wild eyes, riding an exhausted horse. Recognizing the others, the guards waved them through. The group separated; two of them guiding the wild eyed man to Morgan's home, the other heading rapidly to their headquarters. The group with the wild eyed man, upon reaching their destination, dismounted and knocked urgently on the heavy wooden door.

A young man opened the door. "Yes?"

The man in front called out, "We need to see Master Morgan immediately!"

"He IS rather busy, may I ask –"

The wild eyed man lurched forward wringing his hands. "MONSTERS...they took everyone...my...my wife, my children...a whole bunch o' my neighbors, my friends...they took them...." He collapsed, sobbing.

The young man turned pale. "Come in!"

As the group stood in the entryway, the young man turned and opened a door. "Master Morgan, I think you need to hear this."

"Hmph, what is it now? Don't just stand there! Come in."

The group proceeded into the room. "M-master Morgan sir, my name be Don...I...I'm the blacksmith at S'mark village. The...the monsters, they flew down out of the sky...in...in big...boxes! They was little, but they put everybody to sleep...they would wave them...them... claws and people jes fell down! I...I fell against my anvil... and when I woke up they was gone!" He covered his face with his hands. "My...my wife...my two sons. THEY WAS GONE!" He slumped against the wall and slid to the floor sobbing.

Morgan gently touched the man on the shoulder. "May I...look into your memory? Perhaps I can help..."

The man's head jerked up and he made a small warding gesture. "You...you be...one of them...them..." A look of desperation crossed his features. "Yes...anything... anything. Please help me."

At a gesture Morgan's assistant guided the man to a chair. Morgan carefully took the man's hand and looked into his eyes. "Think back to just before...you were in the smithy?" Getting a nod, he went on, "Close your eyes... picture the smithy...the sounds...the smell of the forge... you can feel the heat..." The man's breathing slowed as he began to relax. The guards stared, fascinated, as the two remained motionless and silent for several minutes.

Morgan's face was troubled as he opened his eyes.

"Please find this fellow a place to rest quietly." He said to his assistant. Turning to the other two he said quietly, "Please find Sir Scott and tell him I need to see him as soon as possible. Then return to your barracks and get some rest. He hesitated. "Armus knows?"

"Yes, sir. The others went to report while we brought the blacksmith here."

Subdued laughter announced the arrival of Scott and his guards a short while later. There was a knock on the door and Scott walked in "...So the man said it's SUPPOSED to be brown!" He looked at the man behind him expectantly.

The guard sighed and said, "That's very amusing sir."

Scott chuckled. "You're a barrel of laughs today Karg."

"Whatever you say, sir."

Scott chuckled again. "Go away."

"I'll be outside." The man rolled his eyes as he closed the door.

"Hello Morgan. What's up?"

Morgan gestured toward his study. Scott eyed him silently and followed him into the room. "You look worried. Are you okay?"

"Yes, but something has happened."

Scott sat down slowly. "Okay, talk to me."

Morgan sighed. "I have a blacksmith in the other room who witnessed an attack by monsters that kidnapped people from his village."

Scott's eyebrows rose. He cocked his head to one side and said slowly, "And it looks like you are taking this seriously?"

Morgan took a deep breath. "I examined his memories."

Scott froze. "And?"

Morgan slowly stroked his beard. "I...think you should see for yourself." He rose to his feet. "Please follow me." The two proceeded down a short hallway, where Morgan knocked gently then proceeded through the door into his guest room. The blacksmith lay on the bed. He started to rise, but Morgan waved for him to stay there while he and Scot pulled up chairs to sit by the bed.

Morgan cleared his throat. "Don, this is Scott. The two of us are going to try and find out what happened to your village. May I look at your memories again...and Scott as well?"

The man started. "SCOTT? Are...are ye THE Scott?" He looked like he couldn't decide whether to be awed or frightened.

Scott sighed, "Yes, but don't worry. I just want to know what happened."

The man stared for several seconds before bracing himself. "A' right g'head."

Morgan placed his hand on the man's temple, gestured for Scott to do likewise, then took Scott's other hand in his own. "Okay, Don, try to relax and remember the smithy just like last time...."

Scott made the connection to Morgan's mind, and followed as Morgan accessed the other man's memories. Gradually his view of the room was overlaid by the ghost image of a village. He could see the vague outlines of people walking about. He loosened his mental grip on

Morgan briefly in order to focus on the crystal he now carried at all times, and refocused on the village. It gradually became more clear until suddenly it was as if he was there!

There was some kind of celebration going on in the town square. The sound of a flute drew his attention, and he quenched the horseshoe he was working on and stopped to listen. The other part of him knew that a wedding was taking place, and the couple wearing light blue were the bride and groom. A moment later there was a scream and everyone turned toward the fields. At first, he saw nothing unusual, then movement caught his eye. Coming down the street was a horde of...something...to the astonished blacksmith they were simply monsters. Scott saw what looked like giant crabs, two or three feet tall, each with a pair of large pincers tucked along its sides, and a cluster of small tentacles waving around in front. As Scott focused on the creatures, time seemed to slow and he was able to make out three eyes, two large somewhat bulbous ones toward the sides of the body and one smaller one in the center. As a farmer backed away hastily, one of the creatures seemed to wave its tentacles in his direction and the man collapsed without a sound. Looking closer, Scott could see what looked like a short tube mixed in with the undulating tentacles. Scott saw more and more people fall, although, oddly, the wedding couple, who stood frozen in terror, were ignored. A young girl, also in blue, ran past screaming shrilly. Several of the creatures briefly turned in her direction, their bodies moving back and forth slightly as if searching for something, before continuing on. The blacksmith turned and reached for a large hammer. He tripped, his head glancing off the anvil as he fell behind the forge. The scene went dark.

Scott chewed his lip for a minute before turning to Morgan. "Are there any creatures like that in any of your stories or mythology?" Receiving a definite head shake in response, he sighed. "And they didn't look familiar to you at all?"

"No."

Well...it certainly doesn't seem like something the mind of a blacksmith would invent...." He paused briefly. "Was anyone able to find out if there actually was a wedding there?"

"Not yet, but Armis's people will check. They are also going to see how many are missing and if any trace of them can be found." Morgan held up his hand as Scott started to speak. "Yes, they will check for...strange footprints, claw marks, etc." His mouth formed into a grim line. "I don't like this at all!" He took a deep breath. "What are your thoughts?"

Scott laced his fingers together and said slowly, "I think that since your people came here from somewhere else, I don't see any reason to doubt that there could be other intelligent creatures that don't look like us. Those things were clearly intelligent." He frowned. "From what the smith saw, it didn't seem like they were killing anyone... just knocking them out...although who knows what happened afterwards." His forehead furrowed in thought. "By the way, is there a way for me...us to...see that again without making this poor man live through it again each time?"

Morgan nodded slowly. "Sure. It's your memory now too, so it will just take a simple recall spell. Why?"

Scott was frowning again. "I'm not sure. I just have a feeling that I missed something that might be important."

Morgan shrugged. "Well...it won't take long to go over that recall spell. Let me make sure this man gets some decent sleep, and then follow me."

The following morning, they received a message from Armis stating that about 30-40 people were missing, mostly adults. The ground in the village had been covered with tiny claw marks, as well as something that looked vaguely like human footprints, except they were much too wide. The various markings had converged on a large patch of flattened grass in one of the fields. The wedding party had refused to come to Enimnori, and the guardsmen relayed the impression that everyone they had spoken to seemed to be afraid of "them un-natural folks" and would not be cooperative.

Morgan told the messenger, "See if you can get an exact count of how many were taken, and someone should quietly make sure they have enough resources to get by until we can somehow get those people back." He thought for a moment. "If there are any issues of 'funding' or anything, let me know and I will take care of it personally."

Scott handed the note back to Morgan. "Nuts! I was hoping we could get more information from SOMEBODY. You don't think ANYONE there would help us?"

Morgan shrugged. "Probably not...the blacksmith was still really distraught when he was brought here, otherwise even he probably wouldn't have agreed to it. These people have plenty of time to calm down and...." He spread his hands helplessly.

Scott sighed. "Okay, well I've gone through the scene a bunch of times now, and I think I see something odd –"

Morgan stared at him and burst out laughing. "REALLY? Monsters attacked a village and it took you this long to see something odd?"

Scott scowled at him. "I think the wedding party was invisible to the monsters and I don't think they could hear the children screaming. Yes, I find that odd!"

Morgan shook himself. "Sorry. What do you mean invisible? Those villagers would never use magic! Not even if –"

Scott said sharply, "Not that kind of invisible!" He paused, and then snapped his fingers. "Do you remember when we were talking up there being light we cannot see? When we were making the detectors?"

Morgan's eyebrows rose. "Why yes...yes I do."

"Well, I think that these creatures can't see some of the light that we can, and I think they can't hear some of the sounds we can either." He paused for breath. "You remember the little girl in the blue dress who ran screaming right in front of them without being caught? Well maybe they saw some motion or something like an outline, but they can't see blue, or hear a noise that high!" At Morgan's puzzled look he went on, "You remember the detector that sees heat? Well, if there were, say, a field of rocks that looked the same except one was hotter than the others the detector would let you pick it out, but our eyes would see nothing except another rock...." He paused again. "It isn't exactly the same, but you get the idea?"

Morgan nodded slowly. "I think I understand. But how does this help us?"

Scott slumped in the chair. "I suppose it doesn't right now, but I think it could be important later."

CHAPTER
Six

FOR THE SECOND TIME, A SHINING OBJECT TORE ACROSS THE sky over SMark village trailed by the sound of thunder. It slowed, coming to a stop before settling to the ground in a field a short distance away, there to remain silent. When nothing else happened, the initial panic subsided surprisingly quickly. Heads began to peak from doorways, and finally a trio of men cautiously approached. After a short period of cautious waiting, they relaxed slightly, and backed off toward the village before stopping.

"What is it?" The largest of the trio grounded his pitchfork. "More of THEM...?"

"'Ow the 'ell shud I know?" The second man kept a tight grip on the razor sharp sickle in his hand but lowered it slightly.

The third man shifted a heavy hammer to his other hand before scratching his head. "It be unnatural, that's what it be!"

"Unnatural! That's fer shur...UNNATURAL...." The three men eyed each other in silence, before slowly backing out of sight around a corner. One of them ran to the nearby stable and began to saddle a horse.

~∂ℂ~

IT HAD, AS EXPECTED, TAKEN THE COMBINED EMPATHIC POWER of the entire crew to defuse the sense of panic and replace it with mild curiosity. The idea of sending for help had thankfully come unbidden. The crew watched as one of the bipeds left astride an animal (or something) that looked similar to themselves. There was mild resentment among some of the crew at the obvious fact that their distant cousin was possibly a slave. Examination of the emotional levels of the other similar creatures in the area clearly indicated that they were NOT intelligent, however. The crew was somewhat mollified by the emotions of a much smaller biped who brought food and water to one of the creatures and stroked the animal gently, which the animal found pleasant, even though the small one was itself quite hungry.

Several days passed quietly while the bipeds cautiously resumed their activities and the translator gobbled up enough distant speech sounds to make it happy at last. Finally, a group approached who radiated curiosity and interest. They stopped at the edge of the village and after a brief pause two of them separated from the creatures (horses?) they had been riding and slowly approached the landing craft.

Scott and Morgan stopped about fifty yards short of the alien vessel. Scott regarded it thoughtfully. *Huh, it looks kinda like the space shuttle.* The thought cut off as a door in the side opened and a ramp extruded rapidly. Two creatures came slowly down the ramp. Scott swallowed nervously. *Wow, they look like a squid mated with a centaur.* He recoiled slightly as they came closer. *Holy crap! That beak looks nasty.*

In spite of their bizarre appearance, Scott found himself relaxing and believing that the creatures could be trusted. An internal alarm went off. He and Morgan had both tried to build magical defenses against "mental control" and he sensed a small intrusion. "Morgan! I think these…people… are empathic! Tell me, do you feel like you can trust them?"

Morgan's eyes widened. "Yes, and I sense an intrusion as well. But…I get no sense of threat. Do you?"

"No, and I am feeling quite calm and relaxed!"

"Yeah," Morgan said slowly, "me too."

Hensch661's tentacles twitched in surprise. Unless his senses were faulty then the bipeds had realized their emotions were being manipulated. <shock>*Sir! Calming attempts sensed?*

Tkent412, the commander of the landing force, responded <surprise>*Yes, I see that as well. Amazing! Wait… not frightened…curious!* Tentacles waving slightly, he turned back to the landing craft. *Translator ready?*

Yes sir. Petty officer Jern811 passed the device to the commander, who fastened it in place near his beak. He clicked his beak several times, then began verbalizing. "Hi,

we arrive...peace...no harm. Not monster raid village."
The bipeds froze for a moment. "I Tkent412. What name
you?"

Scott cautiously stepped forward and cleared his
throat. "Greetings. My name is Scott and this," he
gestured, " is Morgan. We can see that you are very
different from those who raided the village." The rippling
tentacles seemed to indicate surprise on the part of the
centaur-like creatures.

"You come now. Not here before. How...know
monsters?" Scott noticed that the voice was coming from a
large box fastened around the torso of one of the creatures.

Scott turned to Morgan and said quietly, "I screwed up!
They CAN tell us apart. Do we tell them? Or should I try
and make something up?"

Morgan sighed. "If they are empathic, then I'm pretty
sure they would be able to tell if someone is lying. Go
ahead and be honest...but you don't have to share
EVERYTHING."

"Right." Turning back, he said carefully, "We used
our...powers...to examine the memories of those who saw
the monsters." The tentacle rippling seemed to briefly
increase. The creature with the box pranced in place for a
moment.

"What mean powers? Mean thing? This thing powers?"
It touched the box with a tentacle.

"Uh...no. We can...do things...different from normal.
We call it magic." He hesitated then slowly and clearly said
several words and turning to the side, made a lifting
motion with his hand. Several feet away a discarded

farming tool slowly rose into the air and hung unsupported. Another incantation and the wooden handle began to smoke, then burst into flames, only to be quickly extinguished. The effect was dramatic. The creatures all took several steps back, tentacles rippling frantically. One of them grabbed an object fastened to its side and pointed it at Scott briefly before lowering it.

"How do? What mean powers? Where thing that make do?"

Scott turned toward Morgan and said slowly, "Did you notice that they don't make any sounds, but act as though they are talking to each other?"

"Now that you mention it, yes"

Scott chewed his lip. "Morgan...I'm pretty sure they are telepathic..."

There was a brief hesitation. "I...am inclined to agree...what are you thinking?"

"That they would react positively to...um...mental communication?"

"WHAT? Are you crazy?" Morgan was horrified.

"I have personal experience with how hard it can be to communicate in a different language...and these aren't even human. Don't forget there are a lot of people who may need help, and these...people may be able to help us but we don't know what the others may do, or how long we have...."

"Huh! Well, I think it is a bad idea, but...." Morgan sighed. "They seem upset already, so...go ahead."

Scott focused on the crystal he always wore now, and began building a mental image of two pairs of cans connected by thin strings. He pictured himself holding one pair with the creature in front of him holding the other pair. *Can you understand me?*

The creature froze, motionless. Scott heard a series of clicks and whistles. He repeated the question. After a brief pause "hear...talk...you?" came from the translator box.

Scott continued to focus. He pictured a microphone connected to a box such as the creature wore. *I am trying to speak to your mind. Can you understand me?*

There was a brief pause, and what seemed like a distant voice answered *I can...please wait...moment.*

The creatures pranced in place for a minute or so, until another of the creatures trotted down the ramp. *I am Mish349...for some...reason I can...understand you very...clearly.*

~ ༠ ༼ ~

SCOTT STAGGERED SLIGHTLY AS HE AND MORGAN WALKED back over toward the village. "I'm exhausted. I'm sorry but can we talk tomorrow?"

Morgan clouded up, then looked closer at Scott. *Wow he really does look bad.* "Just tell me if they can help, then we'll get some rest."

"They are certainly willing to try, I...I think they have some kind of 'in' with someone on the crab-people's ship."

"You mean like a spy?"

"I'm not sure." Scott felt his eyes begin to close of their own accord. "I need to sleep on it."

"Of course, of course. Graham can keep watch."

⁓つC⁓

SEVERAL DAYS PASSED WITH COMMUNICATIONS BETWEEN SCOTT and the "centuaroids" (Minthars) gradually improving.

Scott sighed. "As I understand it, they really want to help but need more time to set things up. I think they are trying to influence one or more of the crew of the other ship, but are having difficulties for a couple of reasons." Running his hands through his hair, he continued, "Part of it seems to be that they think VERY differently, and I think the rest is due to distance and/or not wanting to be detected."

Morgan chewed his lip thoughtfully. "Well, at least they are willing to help. Do they have any idea how long our people will be safe up there?"

"As far as I can tell, they should be safe for quite a while." Scott's voice became harsh and cold. "The crabs are slavers and don't want to damage their new 'merchandise'." His fists clenched. "So aside from being poked, prodded, and terrified, they should be fine."

"So how long are these…horse creatures…going to stay here?"

"They said they have to leave very soon. I think their shuttle," pointing toward the parked spaceship, "is running out of power and won't be able to stay undetectable to the others for much longer. They said that now that they know my…um…I guess 'mental signature' would be closest, they can let me know what is going on, although it might be difficult. I think we should get back and start making what preparations we can." He brightened "Brandon and Geon should be back in just a few days anyway."

Morgan grunted. "I guess you're right. Do you need to say goodbye or anything?"

"I can do that from here."

~つC~

AFTER RIDING BACK IN ENIMNORI, MORGAN HAD ARRIVED AT his home only to find an urgent note from Fredo. Knowing they would get no peace until the "emergency" was solved, they went over to find out what the trouble was. A clearly upset Fredo opened the door at Morgan's knock. "Thank you for coming, I don't know what I would do without you…"

Morgan forced a smile. "What can I do for you?"

"Well, you see, my sister insisted on having a new ball gown for this special party and it had a train…uh…I don't know if you remember, but her husband can't stand Count Krej…"

Morgan nodded. "And?"

"Well, he needed a drink to calm his nerves before going to this party, because Krej was the host. He uh…had a few too many and as they were going up the stairs, he tripped over his wife's gown and fell down the stairs. The message said that he had broken his arm, and I was afraid it might get infected…you know how sickly he is, and, well, I hate to ask, but could you make another poultice and a couple more healing potions?"

Morgan sighed. "Of course, I should be able to have them ready by tomorrow evening."

"Oh, thank you, thank you! You are such a good friend. Our cook is making stew tomorrow, and was hoping you, Brandon and Scott would be able to come over."

"Well, Brandon is not here at the moment, and…"

"Oh! You didn't know? They got back the day before yesterday, he already had a talk with the Count. I think he's waiting in your workroom, he seemed excited about… I can't remember what." He scratched his head. "Something about bats, I think. Anyway, we would absolutely love it if you could come over." He winked. "I have a couple of bottles of good red wine, and I'm sure Frannie would be willing to make cherry pie! You wouldn't want to waste a cherry pie, now, would you?"

Morgan said thoughtfully, "Well it HAS been a while since I had some of Frannie's pie…." He sighed. "Scott?"

Scott hid a smile. "I guess some stew and pie would be nice. We may have to leave early, though."

Morgan nodded. "I'll check with Brandon to see if he is free, but okay…but we REALLY can't stay long."

"Wonderful, wonderful, I'll tell Frannie. She will be delighted, and my wife will be thrilled." He closed the door.

The two of them entered Morgan's home to find a smiling Brandon waiting for them. Noting Morgan's slightly sour expression, he chuckled. "I take it Fredo found you?"

Morgan just looked at him.

Smiling even more broadly, Barndon continued, "Well

anyway, welcome home. It is great to see you both again. Scott..." he said, holding out a bundle wrapped in oiled leather, "As promised, a charged scout weapon, and a new tester!"

Scott smiled back. "Thank you very much!" His expression turned serious. He glanced at Morgan, and receiving a nod went on, "There has been an incident and some surprising developments recently. We have a new problem—"

Morgan interrupted, "Why don't we go sit down? This will take a while."

Seated comfortably in the study, Scott explained the current situation as best he could. Morgan sat quietly as Brandon clearly struggled to understand. "So the crab things... whatever you call them... kidnapped a bunch of people from a village."

"They apparently are known as the Klackari, and yes they did. Morgan was able to view the memories of a local blacksmith and share them with me."

"Okay, and the horse-like things...?"

"Minthars."

"They are enemies of the...Klacks, and want to help us get those people back?"

"Klackari, and...well...they aren't exactly enemies per se, but the Minthars strongly disapprove of what the Klackari are doing, so they are willing to help us. But they insist that any violence be kept to a minimum or avoided if at all possible." Scott paused to collect his thoughts. "It may seem strange, but they are empathic and it REALLY bothers them to see anything being injured or killed."

Brandon shook his head. "That seems...bizarre. "How can they help us if they aren't willing to fight?"

Scott struggled to convey some of the things that had been explained to him on an emotional level, that was somehow both better and worse than words. "Um, they may fight to help us even though they would prefer not to, because they...um...see a great...badness in what the Klackaris do. It sort of causes them a kind of...pain, I guess you could say, to be near anything that gets hurt, but they are all...ah...experiencing something like a constant mental toothache because of all those terrified people."

Brandon scratched his head and shrugged. "Well, as long as they are willing to help us...." He frowned. "What can they do?"

Scott took a sip of wine and sighed. "It's a little unclear yet. I am pretty sure that they have found a way to somehow make some of the Klackari willing to help us. I don't know how, at least not yet. Mish was pretty vague on that issue."

"Mish?"

"Yeah, that's what my new Mithar friend calls himself. Well actually it's Mish349, and no I don't know what that means." He took another sip of wine. "Anyway, they have a way to make their ship sort of invisible to the Klackari, and will take us to the Klackari ship as soon as we can figure out what we are all going to do. They are working on their plan, and we really can't do anything but wait."

"That kind of stinks."

"Yeah, I agree with you Brandon, but," he shrugged, "that just seems to be how it is for now." He shook himself.

"I think I'm going to take a quick look at that weapon, then call it a night."

Morgan cleared his throat. "I am inclined to agree."

Scott awoke with a start, vaguely aware that he had been dreaming, but the details were already fading. He stretched. *Oh, well, as long as I'm up I may as well get something done.* In Morgan's workshop Scott looked over the new things that had been sent from their friends at Land-below; the weapon was obviously old. *Wow! This thing has surely seen better days,* he thought to himself. The battery and charge tester on the other hand seemed to be in fine shape... Idly, he connected the tester to the battery they had vainly been trying to charge...13%..He blinked. *I'm pretty sure they said it was totally drained.* Excitedly, he focused on his crystal, and carefully cast the spell that was supposed to charge it. After about a quarter mark, he let the spell die, and carefully tested the battery again...14%. Grinning broadly, he went to see Morgan.

CHAPTER
Seven

BRANDON SCRATCHED HIS HEAD IN CONFUSION. "I DON'T think I understand."

Scott sighed. "Okay, let me start over. Our brains use electrical signals to control our muscles...."

"I...sort of get that, but what is this thing going to do again?"

"What it does, or least what I hope it will do, is send a large amount of low amperage current into –"

Brandon interrupted. "Sorry, that's where use lost me, what's amp...ampage?"

"Amperage. Um, okay, here's how I think about it...If you picture electricity as flowing water, then the...um... pitch of the flow is the voltage, and the volume..." Seeing Brandon still looking confused, he paused and thought for a moment. "Okay, if you have a wide, deep river that's flowing slowly, then you have a low voltage but very high amperage. If you see a drop of water fall from a roof, that is a high voltage, but very low amperage…"

Brandon nodded slowly. "Okay…."

"Now if you have very high voltage, and also high amperage, that would be like a big waterfall, or a lightning bolt. If you walk across a carpet when it's very dry and touch something, you get a moderately high voltage, but a tiny amperage."

Brandon scratched his head again. "Um…just tell me what it's supposed to do. Maybe I don't really need to know why…?"

Scott sighed again. "Fair enough…what this is supposed to do is make your muscles lock up…um…have a giant cramp…all at once. Most people fall down and start twitching, sometimes they pass out."

Brandon reached toward the now partially charged battery. "Can you show me?"

Scott moved it out of reach. "I have to finish this first," he said, pointing to a rectangular piece of metal with coils of wire on two of the sides.

"By the way, what is that stuff?" asked Brandon, pointing to the wire.

Scott smiled. "It's actually gold wire wrapped in linen."

"WHAT! How in the world did you get that much gold? How much are they paying you…" He trailed off, his face turning red. "Uh, sorry, none of my business."

Scott chuckled. "Don't worry about it. Would you believe Morgan had a gold bar on a shelf in his workshop?"

Brandon said, "Oh…huh! No that's not such a big

shock...Morgan's grandfather owned one of the best wineries in the area. It's easy to forget sometimes, 'cause Morgan doesn't really care about money or fancy clothes or anything like that." He smirked. "Not like Fredo's sister who lives for all that stuff."

"Really? The few times I met him, HE didn't seem like that."

"Oh, HE isn't. He and his wife could really care less about anything fancy. As long as they have someone to help them out, and have plenty of food, they are happy. You should see their house!"

Scott looked up from the wire he was adjusting. "What do you mean?"

Again Brandon smirked. "Let's just say that they aren't going to win any awards for the cleanest or neatest house anytime soon."

"Oh, yeah, I know some people like that. What's the deal with this sister I keep hearing about?"

Brandon frowned and looked around carefully. "I'm not 100% sure, but from what I hear she used to have her eyes on Morgan. I THINK it was because of all the money." He paused. "I don't know if you knew, but Fredo and his sister grew up next door to Morgan's family and supposedly the sister was always jealous because they had a bigger house and fancier things. Well, she finally got her hooks into one of those people that hangs around with the higher ups and gets invited to fancy parties all the time. You know the type, his father was a baron and his mother came from royalty also...so the sister being an overbearing social climber..." He made a vague gesture with his hands.

"Yeah, I get the picture."

"Well, anyway I think it always annoyed her that Morgan just wasn't interested so she was constantly hanging around trying to get his attention, and...uh....let's just say he didn't like it!" Brandon laughed. "So now he lives in terror of her coming back here."

Scott was mostly focused on what he was doing. "Thanks...I think this may be ready." He hesitated. "This is a bit dangerous, so I don't know if I want to test it without Morgan here."

"Why? What's the worst that could happen?"

"If you were born with a weak heart, or if I screwed up really badly, it could kill you."

Brandon looked at the collection of parts thoughtfully. "Ah, what the heck? My heart's fine and I trust you." He took a deep breath. "Let's try it!"

Scott said slowly, "No...I think we should wait for Morgan. He'll only be an hour...sorry, mark or so."

Brandon shrugged and said, "Tell me again what the box thing is for...."

"It's called a capacitor. It stores power."

"Wait, I thought the battery stores the power?"

Scott scratched his chin "It does, but...um...think of it like this: this setup kind of works as if you were pouring water out of a wineskin into a box where you could open the whole bottom of the box at once. It takes a while for the water to pour out of the skin and fill the box, then the box releases it all at once." Seeing Brandon's puzzled expression he was silent for a moment then continued, "Here's another way to think about it; if you take a bunch of gunpowder and make a…uh…trail on the floor, it will take a little while to burn, if you pack it all tightly you get an explosion. It's the same amount of energy in both cases, but one is released faster."

Brandon shrugged. "I don't really get it, but that's okay. I REALLY want to see if this works."

Scott rolled his eyes. "Just be patient."

A short while later Morgan entered the workshop with a rare smile on his face. He hung up his cloak and said mildly, "So…is this the stun device you spoke of?" Indicating the bizarre collection of items on the table.

Scott smiled back at him and said, "Well, yes. This is just a prototype to see if I have everything right. The REAL version will be much smaller."

"Hmm…how are you planning to test it?"

Scott coughed uncomfortably. "Well, I was thinking that I could show you or Brandon how to use it, and you can test it on me –"

Brandon cut him off. "Or you could test it on me. I'm healthy and strong."

Morgan growled, "NO we are NOT testing it on either of you. I know a couple of young strong guardsmen who could use a little extra money. I can just ask for a volunteer." He glared at both of them. "No testing on ANYONE until I get back!" He grabbed his cloak and stalked off.

A short while later, Morgan returned with a slightly nervous looking young man. "Harrison here has offered his services."

Scott said slowly, "Would you like me to explain how it works first?"

The man smiled at him. "Will I understand it?"

Turning slightly red Scott muttered, "I suppose not." Somewhat louder he stated, "It's supposed to give you something like a massive whole-body cramp. It should only last about 5 or 10 beats, but you may fall down...."

Clearly steeling himself the man simply nodded. Scott took a deep breath and poked him with the two sharpened wires while using his other hand to close the circuit. Harrison's entire body convulsed and he crashed to the floor, twitching.

Scott hurried over. "Are you all right?"

There was a brief pause, then "I'm...okay...I think."

Scott said slowly, "We may need to test this a couple more times."

"You mean NOW?"

"No, no, it may take a few days or a bit longer even."

"Oh, okay." The man slowly rose to his feet. Morgan handed him a small pouch and said with a smile, "Thank you very much!"

After hefting the pouch, the fellow nodded and walked somewhat shakily out the door, hesitating briefly to say, "This will help my family a lot. Let me know when you need me again."

"We will," Morgan replied.

Scott smiled and said, "Great, now I just have to make it smaller and neater."

Brandon, looking at the bewildering collection of items spread across the table, said, "How small can you make it?"

"It should fit inside of a hollowed out staff."

Brandon looked astonished. "WHAT, how?"

Scott shrugged. "Well for one thing the plates in that flat box," pointing to the table, "can be basically rolled up, as long as they are separated by a non-conductor like paper."

"Huh, well okay. Can I help at all?"

"Sure...to start with, pass me that thing right over there, and we'll get started."

～⊃C～

THE MAN SEATED BEHIND THE DESK LOOKED PUZZLED. "I'M not sure I understand?"

"It seems that this Scott person has been named as a Journeyman magician." Laughing, Ronn Tracker continued, "He seems to be quite full of himself. He's even started walking around with what I'm sure he thinks of as a 'real wizard staff' with symbols carved on it and everything." He smirked. "I was able to get some of it translated and it worked out to be something along the lines of 'the great and powerful' followed by two symbols that look like a circle and a zigzag."

"...And does this affect our plans?"

"I don't really know. That's why I wanted to talk to both you and Jons." Indicating the third man in the room.

Jons, a former Master magician who had fled Enimnori due to accusations of "unsavory behavior", then shrugged and said disdainfully, "I seriously doubt it. There were no indications that this Scott was even a magician. I suspect that this is merely some honorary thing, so that the magicians can claim partial credit for anything he does." He pursed his lips. "Or just an excuse to give him money or something." He sneered at the other man. "I'm sure the great Ronn Tracker can deal with it. Of course, I will be available to help…in case you find yourself unable…"

"That will be all! Jons, you may go." The magician raised his eyebrows and stomped out.

Looking at Ronn, the man asked carefully. "So…?"

Ronn shrugged. "He may be an ass, but he IS a magician, and should know how they think. I am inclined to proceed as planned, but with a bit more caution."

"Agreed."

ONE EVENING MORGAN CALLED SCOTT INTO HIS STUDY. "Good evening, I have had some thoughts about ways to contact your wife. I think between the two of us we influence her dreams enough to send…impressions."

Scott blinked. "You mean like…uh…'don't be sad', or something like that?"

"Yes, exactly. Then if THAT works, we can try to actually…um…I'm not sure how to put it. Maybe…dream invasion would be the closest."

"What, do you mean? Like me appearing in her dreams and talking to her?"

"Pretty much, yes."

Scott said slowly, "I'm not so sure if that would be a great idea. If she took it seriously and started telling people she could end up being locked up or drugged."

Morgan stroked his beard. "I see your point. Well, we're not there yet anyway. Do you want to try the first thing?"

Scott sighed. "Yes. It would be nice to give her SOME kind of comfort. Do I have to be asleep for this?"

"No, not at all."

"I don't suppose this will be two-way at all?"

Morgan frowned. "Slightly, in the past when this was done the...uh...one sending the dream feelings could, at least in part get a...shall we say impression of how the message was received."

"Okay, I don't have anything else that HAS to be done right now..." Scott raised his eyebrows and made a slight gesture.

"Yes, now would be fine. Okay. Relax, control your breathing and try to link with my mind...."

Scott focussed on his crystal and mentally reached out. *Morgan?*

Morgan's eyebrows shot up. *My goodness! You are really getting good at this. Yes, do you still have your wife's ring?*

Yes, it's right here." Scott slowly reached into his pouch and took out a small leather bag, careful not to break his concentration.

Great! Now focus on the ring and then concentrate on your wife feeling calm and relaxed. I will try to do the rest for now, I can teach it to you later assuming this works...YES, just like that. Now picture your wife, and you should see some kind of a...uh...barrier."

Scott could feel himself starting to sweat as he concentrated. "Um...okay...I...*it looks like a very high picket fence.*

Good, now picture yourself writing a note with a simple message and pass it through the fence.

Scott pictured himself writing "Don't be sad" on a piece of paper and passing it through the fence. The figure on the other side smiled and wrote something on the back. Reading it, Scott felt his concentration shatter. He sat up with a jerk. "Did you see that?"

Morgan shook his head. "No, I'm not really part of the link, I'm just guiding you. I take it you got a response." Getting a nod, "Don't be disappointed if it is cryptic or brief, these things...."

Scott burst out, "It wasn't cryptic or vague. It said, 'Thank you Scott, I know you have been watching.' Morgan, how is that possible?"

Morgan was almost too shocked to speak. "I...I...don't know. As far as I know, you should have only gotten some kind of vague answer if anything." He frowned, "Is your wife particularly sensitive to emotions?"

Scott smiled. "Very much so, and she kind of believes in...I'm not sure how to put it, um, psychic messages, reincarnation, and that kind of stuff."

Morgan said thoughtfully, "This is amazing and almost frightening. Do you feel up to trying again?"

Scott felt himself trembling. "Uh, yes, just give me a minute here..."

Morgan waited patiently until Scott finally managed to regain his focus. "Okay, I think I'm ready."

It took several minutes, but finally Scott once again saw the tall picket fence with the figure on the other side. *Morgan, what happens if I actually try to talk to her?*

Honestly, at this point I have no idea. I...don't think there is any harm in trying.

Taking a deep breath Scott called out to the figure of his wife. *Honey? Can you hear me?* For what seemed like an eternity, nothing happened. Then, *Scotty? Sweetheart, is that really you?*

Scott felt the tears falling from his eyes as he answered, *YES! It's really me. I'm in a different world somehow, I'm safe and okay, but I miss you and the children.*

Where did you go? What happened?

Um, I'm sure you know that the power station was hit by lightning while I was there?

I know, poor Patrick. I feel so bad for Becky, she...

Wait, what? You mean Patrick Higgins? What happened to him?

"Oh dear, you wouldn't know, would you? The whole building blew up and Patrick was killed. He was all burned and...and...broken, it was just awful! But when you weren't there, I just KNEW that something else had happened to you! Dr. Johnson is going to be so surprised...

I don't think you should tell anyone about this. They would think you were crazy.

But...what about the kids? They miss you too, and I think it would make them feel better to know you were safe.

Scott felt himself weakening. *Honey, I have to go now. I'll do this again soon, but for now PLEASE don't tell anyone...not even the children. I love you.*

I love you too. The figure faded. Scott tried to stand, but realized he was too weak. He glanced across the room. "Are you okay Morgan?"

Morgan straightened from his slumped position in the chair. "Yes, what happened? Were you able to communicate with her?"

Wiping away his tears Scott replied, "Yes, it was almost like we were in the same room." He sighed, "I am really tired even though it didn't last very long."

"That's completely normal. You are using a new ability and...well, think of it like exercising muscles you've never used. It will take some time to build up your strength." He brightened. "If this magic amplifier idea of your works it will probably make this easier too." He massaged his neck. "I meant to tell you. I have several of the smaller crystals ready so we can start testing." Looking at Scott's pale face he went on. "I'll start testing. Why don't you try to sleep for a little while?"

Scott stretched. "I guess I COULD use a little rest. If it's okay with you, I'll just take a nap here and meet you in the workroom later."

"That will be fine." Morgan rose to his feet and left, closing the door quietly behind him.

~ ට C ~

LISA HATHAWAY'S EYES SNAPPED OPEN. *WOW, I GUESS I'M more tired than I thought. I don't usually fall asleep in the middle of the day like that. What a weird dream. It seemed so real.* She paused in the act of standing up. *Why would I dream about a picket fence? We never had a picket fence.*

Sitting back down in the living room chair she scowled, deep in thought. *Scott always used to joke about that line from some old poem...'Good fences make good neighbors'....* She gasped! *It NEVER would have occurred to me that Scott wouldn't know about Patrick! I would never dream about picket fences! It WAS a message! IT HAD TO BE!* The more she thought about it, the more certain she became. *That phone psychic was right! He IS in a better place, and he IS watching over me! My Scotty is happy, at least he sounded happy.* Suddenly smiling, she arose from her chair and set out to go shopping with a spring in her step. As she started the car, she reminded herself, *I'll remember Scott, this is OUR secret. Something JUST FOR US!*

CHAPTER

Eight

BRANDON TAPPED ON THE DOOR. "SCOTT, ARE YOU AWAKE yet?"

He was answered by, "Yeah, I woke up a little while ago...I'm feeling much better now. What's up?"

Brandon opened the door and came in. "Morgan told me what happened! It's unbelievable! I don't even know what to say." He took a deep breath. "We're ready to try the magic amplifier idea. Do you feel up to joining us?"

Scott rose to his feet. "Yes, I'm hoping we can make this work. Lead the way!"

With a chuckle, Brandon bowed and made a grand flourish saying, "This way, sir!" The two left and entered Morgan's workroom to see it already set up as Scott had suggested. There were three long tables, each containing several crystals laid out in different ways, and a smaller table holding only a pan of water and a timing candle.

Scott looked at it mournfully. *I've got to come up with a better way of timing things.*

Scott asked carefully, "Did you have a chance to do the benchmark test?" At Brandon's confused look he said, "Sorry, did you time how long it takes to freeze that with and without your crystal?"

Brandon's face cleared. "Bench...mark...I think I get that! Anyway, yes, it takes about 1/20th mark or so with the crystal, and about 1/6th mark without it."

Scott took a deep breath. "Okay. The idea here is to put your crystal in that spot marked on each table. Try again and see if any of these patterns make it go faster."

"Am I supposed to try to tune myself to all those crystals?" Brandon asked.

"I hope not, but unfortunately that's one of the things we may have to test for. I'm afraid this may take a long time."

"Huh. Okay, let's get started." Morgan sat next to the first timing candle with some matches and a notebook.

By the end of the day, they had not had any luck, and Scott somewhat hesitantly asked Morgan if he could try to contact his wife again. Brandon asked if he could help, so the three of them went to Morgan's study. It only took a few minutes before Scott could see the mental image of the picket fence with his wife dimly visible on the other side. *Lisa?*

The figure wavered. *Scott, we are eating supper, and I don't want to frighten the children...unless you want me to tell them, we should wait a couple of hours until they are in bed....*

Okay, I love you.

I love you too. The figure turned away and faded.

Brandon looked at him. "Didn't it work?"

Scott smiled. "It did, but she wasn't alone. Can we try again in two or three marks?"

Morgan said slowly, "That should be fine, but I'm not sure if I need to be here." He looked quizzically at Brandon, who nodded, "I should be able to help now that I've seen how it works."

~つC~

SOMEWHERE IN ORBIT THE TERRIFIED VILLAGERS HUDDLED together in the room they had been herded into when they had first been dragged here. It seemed as though weeks had gone by, but no one had any way to tell for sure. They had discovered by accident that water came out of a small tube in one of the side walls whenever someone was within a few feet of it. The water, which seemed fresh and clear, fell into a depression in the floor that was about five feet long and 3 feet wide. It then vanished through a hole in the floor that could be closed by a metal plate that slid back and forth. The floor on the other side of the large room was covered with a slightly spongy material, while the end farthest from the entrance contained several strange devices, some of which were fastened to the wall.

Periodically a panel would open near the water pipe and several containers of various kinds of meat and plant materials would be pushed through. After a couple of days, one of the bravest (or maybe just the hungriest) of the villagers ate some of the meat, and a couple of the plants that looked similar to normal vegetables. When he still seemed fine several hours later, the rest of the villagers began eating as well.

Shortly after this, several of the creatures entered the room, some of them holding long red metal rods. One of them scuttled forward and extended the pole toward the largest of the villagers. There was a low humming noise and the man fell without a sound. The others backed away. The creature extended the rod again, and the man stirred and slowly sat up, holding his head and moaning softly. Another creature came forward with a rod colored bright yellow. When this touched the unfortunate man, he screamed and frantically jerked away.

Some of the other creatures came forward with similar yellow rods, and with waving pincers and tentacles indicated one of the strange devices on the far wall. Finally, a few of the men walked over to the wall and after further waving of tentacles, started pulling on handles protruding from the wall. Strange symbols glowed briefly on the side of the devices accompanied by sharp clicking and scraping noises.

This became their routine. Some creatures would enter, several villagers would be driven over to the wall and be forced to push, pull or lift things. Sometimes there would be puzzles to solve, such as a box with multiple fasteners that needed to be unlocked in a certain order. Occasionally one or more of them would be knocked out and the creatures would take blood and skin samples. Fortunately, the terrified villagers had no idea of the Klackari's plans to enslave them.

~つC~

AFTER THEY HAD EATEN AND RELAXED FOR A COUPLE OF marks, Scott, assisted by Brandon, made contact with Lisa. This time he was able to maintain the contact slightly longer than on the first attempt, and felt less tired afterward.

Several days later, after successfully assembling and testing his 'taser in a staff', Scott had just finished practicing one of Morgan's complex magical lessons when there was a knock on the door. It was Brandon.

"So, Scott, when do you think we will hear from these horse people?"

His response was a heavy sigh. "I don't know. They said 'soon', but that was quite a while ago, and...." He paused and his eyes went wide. "...I think they are trying to contact me. Quick, link with me and I'll try and uh...'talk' to them."

~つC~

LISA HATHAWAY HAD GONE TO SEE MARIA AGAIN THAT DAY. Seated at the table Maria asked, "Would you like me to try contacting your husband again?"

Smiling to herself, she thought, *If only she knew!* "I'm not sure that –"

"It's okay, dear. I really don't mind. Just close your eyes and picture his face for me."

~つC~

THIS TIME WHEN THE PICKET FENCE APPEARED, THERE WERE TWO people on the other side. Lisa and another woman he didn't recognize. *Lisa? What's going on? Who is THIS?*

The other woman reeled back in shock. *What! Who... what's happening, who are you? What IS this?*

My name is Scott Hathaway...I'm Lisa's husband. Who are you?

I...I...I am Maria Montenegro.

Scott, this is my psychic, Maria. I guess she's really psychic, huh? And to think you thought she was just taking my money!

I guess you're right. My apologies, Maria.

I...that's alright. To be honest, I didn't really know myself, although my aunt was also talking about it. So...are you dead? Is this the other side?

No, I don't think so. As far as I know, I am just in a different world now. One where magic actually works. Lisa can tell you. I was working on some magic, and I'm kind of burned out right now. Sorry but I should go before I wear myself out. I love you Lisa.

I love you too, Scott. The kids really miss you. I wish we could be together again.

Me too, sweetheart. Maybe someday.

~つC~

Lisa opened her eyes. "Now you know why I am feeling so much better. Not only is Scotty NOT dead, but we can really talk. I still miss him, but this helps a lot."

The obviously shaken psychic shuddered slightly and tried to speak. "I...I...you..." She took several slow deep breaths and tried again. "I am...very happy for you. We could be famous, you know...?"

Lisa shook her head. "No, this has to be just between us. At least for now."

The woman sighed. "I guess you're right. There is no way to prove this is real, and they would probably lock us up." She shook herself and smiled shakily. "I think I'm going to close early today...I have some drinking to do." She hesitated. "Will you stay in touch?"

Lisa smiled back. "Yes I will, I promise." With a tentative smile, "You are the only one who can REALLY understand me now."

~つC~

Scott opened his eyes. "Brandon did you see or hear any of that?"

"Sorry, no. Who or what was that?"

Scott laughed, "Do you remember those fake magicians I told you about in my world? Well apparently, the one my wife has been going to isn't completely fake after all!"

"You've got to be kidding."

"Sorry, no." Scott shook himself. "Now, about the amplifier...I'm wondering if it might need something like a wave guide...."

Brandon snorted. "I must have been around you too long. I actually think I know what you mean. Kind of like putting a wall of rocks in a stream so it will go where you want it to?"

Scott laughed out loud. "Yes, exactly. So...let's go find some different kinds of metal bars or blocks."

Two days later, Brandon was grumbling. "Why does it always have to be gold? For once it would be nice to just use some cheap iron for a change."

Scott shrugged. "I have no idea. At this point I am just glad my magic amplifier works at all." He gestured at the item on the table, a flat gold box partly open at one end, containing one large crystal at the open end and several smaller ones in zigzag patterns along the sides. "I sure hope we can cover the whole thing in wood or steel. I don't like the idea of carrying around a gold box."

"Yeah, me neither." He sighed. "I'm glad it's finished. I–"

Scott snorted. "Sorry, but there's a bunch more to do yet."

"What? Like what? It works."

"There are still some things we need to know."

Brandon scratched his head, "Ah! You mean...like... can we make it smaller?"

"Right, and can we use less gold? How close does it have to be to the user? Does it work if it's moving? And probably a few things I haven't thought of." He paused to think. "I think we need to get Morgan involved again."

For the past several days, Scott had been dreaming that a Minthar just kept repeating 'soon'. He quietly cursed to himself. *How soon? Hours? Days? Weeks? You'd think they could do a little better than "soon".*

It had taken the better part of a week, but they had finally determined a few things about the new amplifier. First, a very thin sheet of gold along both sides was enough. Second, the size of the smaller crystals didn't seem to matter, although Scott suspected that there was a bottom limit. Third, the device only seemed to work when the small crystals were exactly an inch apart. Fourth, the "source" crystal could be as far away as 6-10 feet, although the effect weakened somewhat after about 3 feet, and finally, the size of the "exit" crystal seemed to have SOME effect on the size of the output, but not a tremendous amount.

Scott stood looking at the final result, a wooden box about 18 inches long and about 4 inches wide. *It kind of sucks that surrounding it with steel doesn't work...that would be stronger by far.*

Morgan was grinning broadly. "This is an amazing achievement!"

Brandon beamed happily. "Maybe you will be known as 'Scott the amplifier.'"

Scott almost choked on the piece of fruit he was eating. "Yeah, well, not if I have any say in it!" He started to continue, but froze motionless instead. After several seconds he smiled. "FINALLY! They said 'village in two sunrises. Only four.'" He rubbed his hands together. "Let's go tell Wesley and Armis."

Count Wesley was NOT happy. "Four? How are we supposed to mount a rescue with ONLY FOUR PEOPLE?"

Scott sighed, "It's mostly just a matter of size. If we take more than four people there won't be room for all the villagers."

"So why can't they just send more wagons?"

"Shuttles...."

Wesley stopped pacing to glare at him. Forcing himself to calm down he said quietly, "Scott, I really don't care WHAT they are called, just tell them to send more!"

Scott cleared his throat self consciously. "They can't. They said that this ship where they are being held is huge and has a very large crew. This is all about stealth...we need to sneak in, find our people and sneak back out. If we end up fighting, we will lose." Seeing Wesley's expression, he hurriedly added, "We may have to fight them later. If they decide we would be good slaves, they will come in force!"

That seemed to mollify Wesley's bloodlust somewhat. "FINE! Let them try!"

Privately, Scott had serious doubts about winning if that happened. *I sure hope the other part of this plan works.*

～つC～

BRANDON SAID SLOWLY, "SO CAN YOU GO OVER THIS PLAN again? I'm not sure I really understand."

Scott took a drink of water. "Sure, um....well, the Minthars are highly empathic, and some of them are telepathic as well, that is, they can not only read and send emotions, but thoughts also. Some of them took a stealth shuttle and hung around the Klackari ship long enough to...uh...examine, I guess you would say, some of the crew. They found a few that were...um... open to suggestions. They then planted the idea of examining your moons very closely and the crew found out, as the Minthars intended, that the moons are rich in some extremely valuable materials including gold. From there, they kind of nudged a few of them into thinking that they could gain personal glory and wealth by suggesting setting up mining operations, and also selling mining rights to others."

"But...those are OUR moons!"

"Yeah, but they know you don't have space flight so what can you do even if you found out what they were doing? Besides which, they don't care. But anyway, after these guys had decided to do that, the Minthars let a couple of them know that they were here, and told them that if the slaves, which would now just be in the way anyway, were to be released to them that they would then be FAR too busy to report them to the authorities. So the arrangement was made for them to bring a stealth shuttle and get rid of the slaves for them. They will arrange for one of the crew to meet us at an airlock and show us where the slaves are being held."

Clem, one of the senior guardsmen with them, spat on the ground and said harshly, "I don't think we should trust these monsters. ANY of them! How do we know our supposed friends won't betray us and make nice with the others?"

Scott said carefully, "I've been in mental contact with several of them and I am very certain that they won't."

Clem growled, "Fine, I guess, but what about these other...things...how do we know they aren't going to decide that they really just want a couple more slaves?"

"I suppose we don't know for sure, but the Minthars are pretty certain that they think they will get richer faster by getting rid of the slaves and getting started on mining." He shrugged. "We really don't have much choice. Without the Minthars stealth shuttle we wouldn't even be able to get close. Even if we DID have some way of getting there."

Clem sighed, and begrudgingly said, "Yeah, I guess you're right."

Geon said, "As proud as I am to help, I'm not sure what you really need me for. You said there wasn't going to be any fighting, so why bring me and the scout weapon?"

Scott replied, "We certainly hope there is no fighting, and if things go seriously wrong we are screwed and there's really nothing we can do about it. But if things go SLIGHTLY wrong, then having a silent weapon that can kill at a distance could make all the difference. Don't forget, I personally witnessed your skill with it, so...." He spread his hands.

Geon looked determined. "I won't let you down." He paused. "Just one more question. Are you really sure about this? Wouldn't these Klackers be afraid of getting in trouble with their leaders?"

Scott snorted. "Hardly, the captain of the ship gets the lion's share of anything, and apparently thinks slaves are a dirty, smelly, pain in the butt. He is one of the ones that REALLY wants this to happen! He just has to pretend he didn't know."

The ride to S'Mark village was uneventful. They arrived to find a larger version of the ship that had been there last time.

The large stealth shuttle slowly approached its giant target, its cloaking device hopefully preventing its detection. The tension on board was growing with each passing second as the monstrous whale shape grew larger, the flared nozzles of the enormous drives passing out of view as the smaller craft drew alongside.

Brandon felt his stomach churning. *What if that stealth thing stops working?* He looked over at Scott who almost appeared asleep unless you noticed the small rhythmic movements of his hands. *How does he do that? I KNOW he's good at meditating, but...* The thought was interrupted by a sharp CLANG.

Scott looked up and said, "We're there." The next minute seemed to last a lifetime, and then finally with a slight sucking noise the hatch opened.

Scott was already on his feet, his staff gripped loosely in his hands. He turned to Brandon and nodded. They quickly moved through the odd chamber Scott had called an air lock, into a wide corridor that seemed to go on forever. As promised, one of the "monsters" from the village attack was waiting...it waved a claw in their direction and with a series of clicks scuttled off to the right pausing briefly to see if they were following. The four of them followed as quietly as they could.

After several intersections they had traveled deeper into the massive ship and nerves were getting stretched very thin. There was a scratching sound behind them. Scott whirled in a crouch, staff ready, sensing Brandon ready to cast fire and thunder. Nothing...only a fleeting glimpse of something small disappearing around a corner. He felt the touch in his mind again. *CALMLY...IT WAS ONLY A...A... SMALL PARASITE COMMON ON KLACKARI SHIPS.*

Scott motioned to Brandon as he straightened up. He said quietly, "Our friend says it was just something like a rat."

Brandon nodded as he lowered his hands and visibly forced himself to relax. "I wish this was over. How much farther is it?"

Scott shrugged. "All I get is 'soon'."

Another turn in the corridor, more scuttling noises and Brandon's nerves felt like they were stretched to the breaking point.

After what seemed like forever their guide stopped, turned, and began moving its two large tentacles in a complex pattern across a seemingly blank wall.

Even looking carefully, Scott could barely make out faint markings on the wall. The creature stopped and backed away as a door rumbled open. Looking inside Scott could see a large group of people huddled together in the corner, with three VERY large and burly men standing between them and the door. Scott quickly motioned for Clem to come over from where he stood watching the corridor. Clem cleared his throat. "I don't know if you remember me, but my name is Clement Monson. I used to live over in the next town. We've come to take you back home. We bribed a couple of the crab people to let you all go. PLEASE try to make as little noise as possible. If you–" He was cut off by a confused babble of voices.

"Who's that other one?"

"Where are we?"

"I WANT TO GO HOME!"

"Can we leave now?"

"PLEASE!" Clem said forcefully. "Just come with us quietly and–"

The babble continued with one group starting forward, while others huddled against the wall clinging to one another. One of the huge men advanced threateningly. "Ooo the 'ell are you and why shud we trest yeh?"

"I told you, I'm from the next town over. Clem Monson. I really need–"

Pointing at the three watching the corridor the man demanded. "And oo wud they be?" He pointed at Geon and the weapon he was holding. "Wat the 'ell is that bloody thing? It luks pure unnatural to me. We don't cotton to them un–"

Clem made a sharp chopping gesture with his hand. "CUT IT OUT! Do you want to go home, or should we just leave you all here?"

Not getting an answer he turned. "Let's go. They want to stay here!" He only took two steps before several of the people crowded forward. "Wait. WAIT! Don't leave us 'ere with those...those THINGS!"

"Well, come on then!"

The group finally moved into the hallway, several of them fleeing back into the room upon seeing their 'guide'. "It's one of them, they be unnatural."

Scott turned, his temper flaring, "We risked our lives coming here to rescue you. NOW MOVE!"

It took several more minutes to herd them all into a small group. Finally, they started moving. Clem and Scott took the lead with Geon and Brandon following behind. They had almost made it back to the shuttle when two Klackari scuttled out a door that had suddenly opened just in front of them. Scott quickly jabbed one of them with his staff while speaking the word to activate the taser inside it. There was a faint PHZAK and a small, very bright spark. The creature stiffened, then seemed to implode, its legs and tentacles curling in on themselves as it sank to the ground. Its companion tried to scuttle back through the door only to be jammed against the wall by a viscous swing of Clem's mace. It fell motionless in a growing puddle of greenish slime that oozed through its cracked shell.

Scott called out, "COME ON, we're almost there!"

CHAPTER
Nine

THEY ROUNDED THE NEXT CORNER TO THE WELCOME SIGHT OF the airlock. The group ground to a halt. Accompanied by more confused babbling.

"Don't go in there, it's a trap."

Did we go in a circle?"

"Whot the 'ell?"

"I wanna go 'ome!"

"Why are we stopping?"

"Whot's 'appening?"

"STOP IT!" Clem bellowed. "THIS is the way home! Get in there and sit down!"

The crowd reluctantly entered the shuttle and, for the most part, sat in the seats provided with a few simply crouching in corners or against the wall.

The door swung shut with a CLANG, producing a chorus of shocked screaming.

"SHUT UP ALL OF YOU! Everybody sit in one of those seats RIGHT NOW! AND HOLD ON TIGHT!"

Scott 'heard" the pilot. *SHIP ALERTED! LEAVING NOW!* He gripped the seat as the shuttle surged away, the unexpected motion bringing yet another chorus of terrified screams. A message *CLOAK ENGAGING* was followed by a low hum that faded quickly. Shortly thereafter came *CLEAR. SETTING COURSE.*

The ship settled gracefully into the field near the village. The hatch opened and a ramp protruded slowly. The villagers watching fearfully from their homes saw a crowd of people emerge, hesitantly at first, then in a rush as familiar voices called their names. In the midst of the jubilant reunion, four other figures emerged. The ramp retracted and the ship rose silently into the sky, disappearing from view in a matter of moments.

Scott felt a sensation like a silent hug as a fading 'voice' said in his mind, *People returned...happy. Glad to help...will monitor ship.*

Scott was chatting with Brandon when the blacksmith, followed by the village leader, slowly walked over. "I... we...we thank ye." The blacksmith looked at the ground briefly before taking a deep breath and extending his hand. "We was wrong about ye. Ye may be unnatural, but ye dun a gud thing. Be well...friend." He shook Scott's hand, reddened slightly and turned, walking back toward the village. The other man met his eyes and said, "We're beholden' to ye, if ye ever need us...well...unnatural or not, jes send word."

Scott smiled and turned to see Clem staring at him. "What?"

Clem looked astonished. "THAT was almost as amazing as the rescue. These people NEVER admit making a mistake about things like that. Armis was right. You are truly a phenomenal person, and I am honored to know you."

Turning red, Scott replied, "I'm nothing special. I just did what anyone would do."

Clem snorted. "Right, and anyone can stop a monster just by poking it with a stick too! I'll get the horses." He started walking toward the stables shaking his head.

As they were mounting their horses, several children ran up to them heavily laden. The four of them were presented with a large pot of stew, several loaves of bread, 2 horseshoes, a bag of cut nails, 4 freshly sharpened knives and several hand woven scarves. Clem dismounted and gratefully accepted on behalf of all of them. "Many thanks young'uns, and please tell your folk that these gifts will be truly cherished."

The oldest, a girl who looked to be about fourteen grasped Clem's hand, looked into his eyes, said, "My pa says ta tell ya that...I be marriageable come next year." She dropped her eyes, and blushing, ran back to the others. Clem turned bright red and waved awkwardly, as Brandon began to chuckle.

Arriving back at Enimnori was anticlimactic by comparison, with the guards simply saying hello and waving them through the gate. They quickly passed through the town itself and immediately went to the castle to inform Count Wesley and Armis of their success.

The Count's chatelaine, who had apparently been given notice of their pending arrival, greeted them with a broad smile and personally escorted them directly to the Count's audience chamber. Wesley rose to his feet expectantly. "Good news I hope...."

The others nudged Scott forward and he quickly informed the Count of what had transpired. Finishing with, "...So then the villagers gave us a couple of gifts and we came back here."

Clem burst out. "They not only gave us gifts, the Headman came over, thanked Scott personally and even shook his hand!"

Wesley's eyebrows went up. "Are you serious? WELL! Huh, I don't suppose he went so far as to admit being wrong about all this 'unnatural' business?"

"No, not exactly. He just kind of allowed that not all of us are pure evil."

Wesley sat back down. "That is still quite a concession. I KNOW that stiff necked old bigot, and usually he would rather cut off his own arm rather than admit being mistaken about ANYTHING!" He snorted. "Well done... ALL of you...very well done!"

Morgan was pleased. "I must say that worked out splendidly, and you say the villagers actually admitted that you weren't evil?"

Scott snorted. "Yeah, I don't know if it extends beyond the four of us, though. They also offered to help if we ever needed it."

Morgan scowled. "Huh, that may almost be more along the lines of repaying you so they don't have to feel grateful anymore." He brightened. "Or maybe they really mean it the way most of us would."

After a good night's sleep, Scott, Morgan and Brandon met in the workroom. Scott spoke enthusiastically. "Now, it seems like we're getting an amplification factor of around four or five to one with this setup. What I would like to do next is see if they can operate in tandem." He took a breath. "How soon can we get another of these ready?" He scratched his head and continued eagerly, "Maybe two would be better! Then we can–"

Morgan interrupted. "Wait. You want two MORE of these things?" he said incredulously.

Scott and Brandon continued testing the magic amplifier while Morgan somewhat grudgingly had some craftsman make and supply the parts for two more. Scott had gone to the kitchen to get them some bread and cheese one day, only to return to see Brandon scratching his head.

Brandon looked troubled. "Scott, I tried the amplifier again while you were gone and it didn't work."

"What? Did the crystals get damaged somehow?"

"I don't know."

"We better check." Scott opened the box carefully. "Everything still LOOKS okay...nothing is out of place either." He scratched his head. "Let me...uh...watch...." He activated what he thought of as his 'magic eye'. "Okay, go ahead...." After a brief pause, Brandon gestured and the 200 pound block of lead rose into the air. Scott looked at Brandon who shrugged and said,

"Maybe you moved something when you opened the box?"

"I didn't think so...." Scott reclosed the box and nodded at Brandon. The block rose again.

It was Scott's turn to look troubled. He frowned. "NO! It couldn't be...."

"Couldn't be what?"

"Um, Brandon can you just hold it there for a while please?" Scott slowly began to back out of the room. As he reached the door about 20 feet away, the box began to wobble. He began moving down the hall, stopping when he heard a strangled voice behind him. "I can't hold it any more." Scott walked quickly back into the room, only to see the block shoot toward the ceiling, stop and hover again before lowering to rest on the table.

Scott walked over to a stool and sat down heavily. "That's not good," he said glumly. "Why in the world would it act like that?"

Brandon snorted. "I guess it likes you."

Scott glared at him, then blinked. "Wait, you've used it before without me in the room, haven't you?"

Brandon thought for a moment. "No, actually I haven't."

Scott said heavily. "I think it's time to talk to Morgan again."

Morgan was shocked. "That...doesn't seem possible. Are you sure?"

Scott sighed. "Yes, we are pretty sure. It only works when I am close to it...about 20 feet or so." He brightened suddenly. "Hey, maybe another magician needs to be present, but it doesn't matter who." Looking at Morgan. "We could test that pretty easily."

They all went to the workroom and found that not to be true. For some reason the amplifier would only work in Scott's presence. He began pacing back and forth. "There HAS to be a reason for this, but I can't seem to think of one right now." He looked over at Morgan and Brandon. "How about you two, any ideas?" Both men shrugged.

~つC~

THIS TIME, BY USING THE AMPLIFIER, SCOTT WAS ABLE TO contact his wife without any help. *Lisa, darling, how is everything? Sorry it's been a while, but we have been busy and tired. We managed to make a...device...that amplifies...I mean makes magic stronger. I can contact you by myself now without bothering the others. It still makes me tired, but it's getting easier. Are the kids still okay?*

Well, I'm a little bit worried, especially about Gwen. She doesn't like high school. Some of the girls are teasing her about being a geek. One little brat even had the gall to hint that you disappeared to get away from her...she...uh slapped the girl and the parents are talking about pressing charges. I know we'll get through it somehow, but it's hard.

I'm so sorry I can't be with you. I'm not happy that she's in trouble, but sort of glad she stood up to the girl. Did anyone else hear what was said? Maybe if you talk about suing for defamation or something, they would either understand or back off. I don't know if you remember, but Freddy studied law for a while, he might be able to give you some advice.

OH, that's right, I remember now...I'll call him and ask. Thanks honey. You look funny, is something wrong?

I think I'm just kind of tired, this is harder than I thought it would be, even WITH the amplifier. Good Bye for now. Remember, I love you.

I love you, too!

⁓ↄc⁓

BRANDON AND SCOTT WERE ONCE AGAIN IN MORGAN'S workroom. The parts had arrived late the day before, and Morgan had assembled a second amplifier.

Brandon set the box down where the other one had been, put his crystal in front of it and focused on the large block of lead. Nothing happened. He blinked, looked at it and concentrated. The block slowly rose an inch or so, while sweat beaded his forehead. He relaxed and the block thudded back down. He looked at Scott who frowned, slowly walked over and carefully opened the box. "Everything looks fine." After staring at the box for a while, he looked at Brandon. "Any thoughts?"

"Actually, yes. You assembled the first one and it only works when you are here. MORGAN assembled this one...."

Scott blinked. "You know, that may be it. I hate to bother Morgan again, but...."

After a brief discussion, Morgan had Brandon assemble the third device, and they returned to the workroom. It didn't take long to confirm Brandon's idea that, for some reason, whoever actually assembled the amplifier had to be nearby in order for it to work.

Scott said, somewhat forlornly, "That's…very strange. I'm really sorry…."

Morgan laughed out loud. "Sorry for WHAT exactly? It works just fine. It sometimes happens that magic items only work for their creators. No one has ever been able to figure out why, but it isn't a big deal." He clapped Scott on the shoulder. "I know you always want things to be perfect, but this is…I don't even know how to say it. This is potentially an enormous discovery, and you should be proud of it."

Scott, looking embarrassed, said, "I guess you're right." He straightened his shoulders. "OKAY! Now, let's see if these things are additive."

It took the rest of the day to verify that one device would indeed feed another device and the result was more than a twenty fold increase in power. They were also able to channel the output of two amplifiers to feed the third, but the output results were disappointing, showing only a slight increase at the end. Trying to use three in a row actually resulted in a REDUCTION of power!

"Well, THAT was unexpected!" This time it was Morgan who was disappointed. He looked over at Scott who seemed lost in thought. "What are you thinking about now?"

Scott rubbed his chin and said, somewhat distantly, "I…was wondering if we could try sending my wife's ring back to her. The two of us are obviously strongly linked, and the ring being quite small...." He looked at Brandon somewhat pleadingly.

Brandon nodded sharply. "I'm certainly willing to try. Did you want to try it now?"

"Ah...no, I think I should warn her first. Then we can eat, rest and try it a little later."

~ɔc~

LISA? ARE YOU THERE?

I'm here Scotty.

In a couple of hours, we are going to try sending your wedding ring back. We don't know if it will work, but it seems like something worth trying.

That should be fine, Danny is across town and Gwen has a cold and is going to go to bed early. What do you want me to do?

I think if you sit on our bed and think about us doing things together, that may help.

I can do that, I do that a lot anyway. It won't take me more than an hour or two to clean up the dishes and get Gwen settled.

Great! Now don't be upset if it doesn't work.

Well, I may be a little upset, but like you said, it's worth trying.

~ɔc~

THE FIRST TIME THEY TRIED IT NOTHING SEEMED TO HAPPEN except for Brandon developing a headache. Then Scott contacted Lisa with Brandon using his amplifier. Scott, standing next to the mental picket fence saw a brief flash of what looked like heat lightning and Lisa screamed *IT'S HERE! IT'S HERE! The bed in front of me looked kind of... wavy for a second and then there it was right in front of me!*

Wow! That is great. I have to talk to the others now, but this gives me hope.

"Brandon, are you okay?"

"Um...yeah, I'm just a little tired and I kind of have a nasty headache, but I think I'll be fine in the morning."

It was a couple of days later that Morgan had invited his friend and fellow magician Valtir to come and see the new magical amplifier. They were discussing it when there came an urgent knocking at the door. A moment later Morgan's newest apprentice entered the workroom. "Master, your neighbor Fredo is here to see you. He claims it's urgent."

Morgan sighed, "Very well, show him in." He shrugged at Valtir who grinned at Morgan's obvious annoyance.

"Morgan...Morgan. I'm so sorry to bother you." Fredo was wringing his hands. "My wife...she can't stop throwing up...I...I tried giving her brandy, but it just seemed to make it worse –"

Morgan held up his hand to stop the flow of words. "Slow down. Take a deep breath and tell me when and how this started."

Fredo forced himself to take several shaky breaths before continuing in a more normal tone. "I'm not entirely sure. My wife had gotten hungry and decided to finish a special dish Frannie made yesterday."He frowned slightly. "I can't remember what she called it...anyway, I know it was made with whipped oil, eggs and chicken, or maybe it was whipped eggs. It was really good, Morgan, you'll have to try some sometime, but, well…it wasn't even a whole mark later when Burtha started throwing up."

Morgan got up and crossed the room, rummaging through some cans, he poured something into a small empty wineskin, which he brought over and handed to his friend. "Here, have her drink a little of this every few minutes until it's gone. I think that will help. Oh, and I would throw away any of that dish you have left."

Fredo hurried away, calling over his shoulder, "Thank you SO much. I don't know what we would do without you!"

Morgan turned back to Valtir. "Where was I?"

"I believe you were just about to explain the assembly process. But first I am curious what you gave him."

"Oh, that. It is a special blend of herbs, powdered charcoal and calcium carbonate. It should help settle her stomach and also should help with the…um…next phase of the problem, if you get what I mean."

Valtir looked puzzled. "Next phase?"

Morgan sighed. "Let's just say that what doesn't come out one way will probably come out another way."

Valtir snorted. "Oh, sorry I asked. Now, you said there was something odd about this assembly process?"

"Oh, right! Well it turns out that the final assembly should be done by the person who is going to be the primary user because it will only function in his presence."

Valtir grunted. "So…others can use it if he or she is nearby?"

"Correct, within about 20 feet or so."

"That doesn't seem too restrictive. You said there was a catch...."

Morgan handed him a piece of paper. "Yes, well it takes 8 small crystals and one large one, and two of the plates have to be made of gold...about an ounce or so each."

Valtir burst out laughing. "NINE crystals, AND two ounces of gold? I guess we won't have to worry about these things proliferating!"

Morgan smiled slightly. "No, I don't think that'll be a problem. That may be just as well. I'm not sure how many people I want to know about this, at least for the time being."

Valtir looked down at the piece of paper in his hand. "The rest of this seems pretty straightforward. I'd better get back. Thanks for this." He headed for the door, muttering under his breath, "Nine crystals and two ounces of gold."

CHAPTER

Ten

MARTIN DENER FELT LIKE TEARING HIS HAIR OUT. "WHAT happened? I knew that Franz was going to cause trouble sooner or later after he was deposed. How long has he been gone?"

"It's only been one day and…." His second in command and good friend Winston paused. "Technically we don't really know that this is HIS doing."

Martin said sourly, "Jake is almost never late, and now no one seems to know where he is. I really don't think that it's a coincidence that this happened two days after that mysterious letter appeared claiming I was conducting," he picked up a piece of paper, "unnecessary and dangerous experiments." He snarled and threw the paper down. "How can I even respond to that?"

His answer was a shrug. "Well, I still think we should just ignore it…if we seem to be taking it seriously then we just give credence to it."

"Blast it, I suppose you're right." He slammed his hand on the table. "OW...If only there was some way of telling who was behind...." he broke off seeing a sudden change of expression on his companion's face. "What?"

Winston said slowly, "Our magician friends can sense emotions...."

Martin sucked in his breath. "That's RIGHT! I had forgotten...." He pushed a button on his desk. "Frank? Would you please have someone locate ambassador Varney and ask him to stop by at his earliest convenience...thank you...what? Which group? No, not today...see if you can make an appointment for ...." He looked at the viewscreen on the side of his desk. "Tomorrow about 10:00 or," moving his finger across the screen, "the day after shortly before or after dinner...yes... okay, great, thanks. Please inform me as soon as Varney is located." Tapping the button again, he said, "Thanks Winston, I should have thought of that myself."

"Well, I DID spend a lot more time with them...."

Winston seated himself while Martin continued his onscreen 'paperwork'. There was silence for several minutes.

Finally, there was a beep. Glancing down, Martin tapped the button on his desk to speak to his assistant. "Yes?"

"Ambassador Varney is on his way. He should be here in a few minutes sir."

"Oh, alright I can see him now. Please show him in when he arrives."

A short while later there was a knock on the door,

which opened to admit Master Magician Varney, Ambassador from Enimnori. After nodding politely to both men, he entered and, at a gesture from Martin, sat in the chair next to Winston. He tilted his head and raised his eyebrows in question.

Martin cleared his throat. "We have had some unrest lately which we believe to be the work of those in the employ of Franz Serif, the former resident of this office," he said carefully. "After his disappearance following last year's regime change, we have seen absolutely no sign of him. However, we are certain that he has remained active in the background, simply biding his time while his agents attempt to create a climate conducive to his return." He smiled. "It occurred to us that in the past you demonstrated the ability to...ah...locate persons with hostile intent toward a given subject?" At Varney's nod he went on, "We were hoping we could impose on your abilities to find at least some of those who are causing these disruptions."

Varney thought briefly before responding. "I believe that lies within the scope of both my authority and abilities. What did you have in mind?"

~つC～

BRANDON ENTERED THE WORKSHOP AND EXCLAIMED excitedly, "Scott...Scott, guess what! We've been invited to come along for the annual Rock Glorban harvest! I've always wanted to go, and now that we are famous I thought I would ask again...and THEY SAID YES." He took a breath. "Can you come? You're not too busy right now, are you?"

Scott blinked. "Glorban...Oh, you mean like that glorban stew the Count had for us when we got back from Dener peak?"

"Yes, exactly! Well, the glorbans are only available in a few places, and only for less than a month out of the year. We would be leaving in about a week or so. You can come, right? Please tell me you can come!"

Scott hid a smile. "Well, I don't know Brandon. I would like to but..." He pretended to frown. "I probably should check with Morgan, and also make sure that Armis or The Count don't need...." He stopped as Brandon's face fell, then laughed. "I'm kidding. I'm sure it will be fine. I could use a break anyway. Shall we inform Morgan?"

Several days later, with the planning complete, the party set off. Aside from the usual group of drovers, work-men, and guards, there was a group of about a dozen 'dig-nitaries' who were just along for the ride. It was an uneventful and quiet trip, despite some of the other guests who seemed like they just HAD to talk constantly, and apparently felt it was their duty to fill Scott and Brandon in on all of the gossip they might have missed.

Scott was riding in a partial daze, with an attentive half smile on his face the day they arrived. His current trav-eling companions were an older, slightly paunchy fellow and his wife. Scott forced himself to pay attention. "So the ball ended sooner than expected, you said Sir Jonce?"

"That's right, young fellow. You see the ice they had brought to keep the food fresh melted sooner than expected...a LOT sooner, and, well it being a hot day and all...um...." He coughed delicately. "Let's just say that some of the food might have...um...shall we say, aged less than gracefully, and several of the other guests were having...DIFFICULTIES...." He waved his hands as though shooing away the unpleasant memories. "It was VERY embarrassing for the poor hostess, and then to top it all off–" He was interrupted by some shouting from the front of the column. "Are we stopping so early?" He raised up in the stirrups and shaded his eyes. "OH! Wonderful. We have arrived. Will you excuse me Scott? I really should make sure our tent is set up properly this time. I don't want a repeat of what happened two days ago! My poor wife barely slept a wink."

"Oh, that's quite all right. Perhaps I will see you later." *Yeah, if I can't avoid it, you old blowhard,* Scott thought to himself as they left.

Brandon rode over with a smirk on his face. "I'm so sorry I had to go check on the ice. We wouldn't want the food to go bad...some of the group might have DIFFICUL-TIES and that just WOULDN'T do." He sniffed into an invisible handkerchief.

Scott snorted. "Yeah, thanks Brandon." He squinted, then used a small telescope (one that he and Brandon had so laboriously created soon after he had arrived on this world) to look ahead. "Wow! That is quite some gorge!" Sweeping the telescope back and forth he commented, "Is that as narrow as it looks over that way?" he asked, pointing to the east.

"Yes, you know that REALLY long wagon?"

"Yeah, I keep forgetting to ask about that."

"Well among other things it includes a bridge, after one was destroyed in a storm a while back. They just take it apart and ship it back and forth each trip." He shrugged. "After all you have to have SOMETHING in place so people can get in and out of the gorge quickly. You know how it is," he said, giving Scott a sidelong glance.

Scott sighed. "No Brandon I DON'T know how it is because nobody will tell me!"

Brandon said, "Well, strictly speaking I don't exactly know either, because I never got a chance to see it before, but they say it's pretty spectacular."

"WHAT is spectacular? Why doesn't anyone want to tell me?"

"Honestly, I think they find it amusing that the great Scott doesn't know something."

"Okay, and why won't YOU tell me?"

Another smirk. "I wouldn't want to spoil the...wait... IT'S TIME!" He scrambled quickly off his horse and began running toward the gorge. "COME ON!"

With a deep sigh, Scott also dismounted quickly and followed Brandon over to where most of the group was lined up along the gorge, talking excitedly. Everyone was staring toward the west. *Hmm they said the ocean is only a few miles from here. I wonder....* His thought was interrupted by a distant low rumble that grew rapidly louder. Scott's jaw dropped as the reason for the noise became clear. A wall of water at least 30 feet high came roaring UP the river about as fast as a galloping horse. Scott watched open mouthed as the flow rose another 10 feet at least upon reaching the narrow channel. "Holy crap." He turned to Brandon. "That really is amazing! How often does that happen?"

"Uh...on a smaller scale, a couple times a day maybe, but the bigger ones like this only happen, I don't know, every couple of days, more or less. In most rivers, it's only a few feet high, but something about this river...." He shrugged. "Don't know if anybody really knows why, although it has something to do with the moons I think."

Scott looked up at the two moons which were very close together in the sky. "Yeaaah, okay. It's a tidal bore."

Brandon stared at him. "Don't tell me you understand this too!"

"Only partially. It has to do with the gravitational pull of the moons. As I understand it there would be a much stronger effect when the moons are close together," Scott said, pointing at them. "And even more so when they are lined up with the sun...er...Day Sphere."

"So...if the moons are on opposite sides of Varushna, they would, um, pull the water...both ways, and nothing would happen, right?"

Scott scratched his head and said slowly, "I don't think so." He paused, frowning. "If I remember right there's a... um...water bulge on both sides of the planet, so they would only cancel each other out if they were perpendicular."

Brandon sighed. "Perpa what?"

Scott chuckled. "Sorry, um...." Looking around, he bent and picked up two sticks and holding them in a cross shape, and said, "The two sticks are perpendicular, so if

Varushna is at the center here, then when the moons are at either end of the sticks, THAT'S when they...uh...act against each other."

Brandon looked at the sticks for a moment before shaking his head. "I still don't think I get it."

Scott thought about it. "I...don't really understand it well enough to explain why, but I do know that that's the way it works." He shrugged. "Sorry."

That evening Brandon came to their tent after having spent a little while chatting with the magicians who had been hired for security and food safety (keeping the perishables cold). He was feeling both angry and smug. *I did this by myself, and it still takes three of THEM! I know Morgan tells me I should be more patient with people who aren't as strong as I am, but these guys are patronizing ME. Ah well...* He stopped, seeing Scott's face and sat down slowly. "Um...hi. What's up?"

Scott took a deep breath. "Oh, I'm alright. I was just in contact with Lisa, and my children are having some problems. My daughter says she doesn't like school any more, and my son is starting to hang out with people that are best avoided, if you know what I mean."

Brandon grimaced. "Yeah, I think I do. I guess jerks are jerks no matter what world you are from."

Scott shook himself and tried to smile. "Sorry, I don't mean to bring you down. I know this is your big adventure. So...how are things with your colleagues?"

"Well, if your son was here you probably would want to keep him away from them."

"Oh, I see. Sorry about that."

"Eh…no a big problem. Trust me, I'm not going to let a couple of florfs like them spoil my trip! I thought at first they were just busy and stressed because of all the fancy people here, but I guess it's just the way they are."

"Uh, Brandon…what the heck is a 'florf'?"

"Oh, sorry. It is….well, kind of a hmmm…low class person who is too ridiculous to be bothered with."

"I see, I might call them 'dweebs'. Seems like about the same thing. Oh by the way, maybe it's none of my business, but why are there three of them? I thought you managed all this by yourself?"

Brandon grinned. "Well, let's just say that not all magicians are created equal. These losers got the job because their parents are rich and have friends in the right places, not because they are good at what they do!"

That got a laugh. "Yeah! Sadly enough, I know exactly what you mean." He shook his head. "I guess that's universal too…it's not what you know, it's who you know." He yawned. "Ah well, tomorrow is another day. Sleep well."

"You too, thanks. Good night Scott."

"Good night."

The rest of the trip was relatively uneventful, although one man had to be rescued after staying a little too long while trying to harvest one last glorban before the tide came back. The fellow in question had been having a hard time digging a particularly large glorban out of its lair in the rock wall, and hadn't wanted to give up. This was in spite of the warning system they had in place, which consisted of a man about a mile downriver with a huge trumpet, and two others equally spaced between him and the harvest crew. Their jobs were to blow the trumpets as soon as they saw the tide coming in. When the first trumpet sounded you had about a minute and a half warning, with the other two giving roughly a minute and a half minute, respectively.

Scott privately thought the creatures looked disgusting, and was shocked at the memory of just how good that stew had been. *I kinda wish I hadn't seen these things. They look like a cross between a giant, slimy centipede and a scorpion. No wonder those guys all wear those thick gloves. It may be a while before I eat glorban stew again!*

The group was riding along on the way home when Bandon pulled up alongside Scott and said quietly, "I wonder how Morgan's doing."

Scratching his head Scott said quietly, "Probably okay. As long as the vineyard is running well and Fredo doesn't have any crises, he should be fine."

Brandon smiled. "Yeah, I guess you're right. How are things with your wife? I know you talked to her last night."

Scott shrugged, "Well, she seems to be doing okay. Her yoga business has picked up but the kids are still having some trouble in school."

"What kind of trouble?"

"Well it seems Gwen is still being picked on a lot. I'm not quite sure what's going on with my son, just that he isn't doing well. Lisa didn't really want to talk about it." He sighed, then went on, "I am eager to get back. I have a couple of..." He paused and his eyes went distant.

Brandon looked at him sharply. "What is it?"

Scott held up one finger and Brandon waited until Scott refocussed his eyes and said with a smile, "That was a little freaky. The Mithar's are in a heavily cloaked ship a couple of miles up, and just wanted to tell me that apparently the mining thing caught on big time with the Klackari and they have abandoned all thoughts of slave trading, at least for now." He rolled his head and massaged his neck before continuing. "He said they will always keep a ship of theirs in orbit as long as the Klackari are here."

Brandon smiled. "You know, as ugly as they may be, they really are nice people, aren't they?"

"Yeah, I think so, too!"

A somewhat dusty Scott knocked politely on Morgan's door before entering. He was met by a slightly wild-eyed servant who simply grimaced and waved before disappearing into one of the rooms. Walking down the hallway, he heard a familiar voice snarl, "WELL! Who is it and what do they want?"

Scott walked into Morgan's office and said with a fond smile, "It is merely Sir Scott of Enimnori here to seek an audience with– "

Morgan scowled at him. "Alright, alright. What is it?"

Scott said slowly, "It's been a bad day, I take it?"

Morgan regarded him grumpily for a moment before relaxing somewhat. He said with a sigh, "Yeah, you could say that. First I get some disturbing news from Varney in Landbelow, then Fredo comes in wanting another of his stupid healing potions, and before he even leaves, my foreman comes in with the news that there's some kind of blight in the southern fields! HERE!" He snapped handing Scott a small clay vessel. "Please take this over to Fredo and tell him I said to stuff it down his–"

Scott interrupted. "Maybe I should just tell him that his potion is ready."

"Fine, do as you please!" Morgan stalked out the door, turning briefly to snap, "Welcome back!"

Scott chuckled to himself as he went to deliver the potion to Morgan's neighbor and frequent 'thorn-in-his-side'.

Later that evening Scott asked a still disgruntled Morgan, "What's happening with Varney?"

Morgan steepled his fingers and grunted. "Huh. Well, it seems he is getting a little involved with the local politics. Apparently, the deposed ruler..." he raised his eyebrows at Scott questioningly.

"Um, Franz Serif."

"It seems that he has been spreading rumors and trying to stir up trouble. Varney has been pressured into becoming the local traitor finder, if you can believe that."

Scott nodded. "Yeah, this guy Martin isn't shy about getting people to do things for him."

"Do I hear a trace of disdain in your voice?"

"Well, maybe a little. We had words a few times and let's just say he isn't used to hearing the word 'no'."

Morgan snorted. "Yeah, well a lot of rulers get that way, if they weren't already. Sometimes Wesley...never mind. Anyway, now that Varney has identified a bunch of suspects, this Martin person wants him to interrogate them as well, and didn't like it when Varney said that would be inappropriate."

Scott said slowly, "Oh yeah! I can just imagine that conversation." He laughed. "I expect Varney's one and two word answer style didn't make him too happy either."

Morgan took a large drink from his cup. "Ahhh." Setting the cup back down he went on, "Yes, while Varney didn't really say so, I suspect you are correct." He scowled again. "Even if we WANTED to help it would take months to get there, and...WHAT?" He recoiled a bit at the somewhat wolfish smile that began to spread across Scott's face. "What are you thinking?" he asked almost fearfully.

Scott smiled even more broadly. "The Mithars could get us there in less than a day."

"THE MINTHARS! You...you mean those horse things?"

"Yes. They contacted me on the way home to let me know that the plan worked and that they would be watching over us at least until the Klackari go away."

Morgan scowled again. "Much as I hate depending on those things, they DID help us before when they didn't have to. Maybe next time they...talk...to you, you can ask them. Then at least we'll know if it's even possible." He shuddered slightly. "They still creep me out though."

The following morning Scott took 'his' amplifier and decided to try contacting the Minthar he knew best. After setting up and clearing his mind, he focussed on the amplifier, and concentrated...*Mish749...can you hear me?* He tried several times, and finally:

<surprise> Yes. Is this Scott-human?

Yes! I wanted to see if I could call you. Am I disturbing you?

No...resting.

Are you aware of a second smaller group of people near this mountain <mental picture of Dener peak>

Yes...emitters of sporadic week EM signals there. Occasional strong signal.

Yes well, we left an...emitter there to speak to our friends.

<confusion>

It's kind of a long story, but we are...friends...and they might be having trouble someday. Would it be possible for us to get a ride on one of your shuttles if we needed to get there quickly?

<surprise> Possible...may not be allowed...must ask...will contact with answer.

Scott blinked as the contact faded he looked around and saw that Brandon had come in while he was concentrating. "Oh, hi. What's up?"

Brandon gave him a look. "I was just going to ask you that," he replied, looking pointedly at the amplifier. "Anything I can ask about?"

"Oh, sure. I had a thought the other day that maybe the Minthars might be able to give us a shuttle ride if we ever needed to get to Landbelow in a hurry. I– "

"Wait..." Brandon's eyebrows went up. "You mean those ugly horse-like things with the...uh...funny arms and the snakes on their heads?"

Scott sighed. "Brandon...."

"Yeah, yeah. I know, they're our friends, be respectful. But that is how they look!"

"I suppose. Anyway, the one I know best is going to check and see if it would be okay."

"Hmmm, you know, it sure would beat the hell out of riding for months."

Scott chuckled, "Yeah, that's what I thought. Especially if we needed to hurry. Anyway, he said he would check and let me know."

"Great! You said earlier that there was something you wanted to talk about?"

Scott reached into a drawer and pulled out two pieces of paper. Putting the first one in front of Brandon, he said, "This is what my people call a pendulum clock. Now, I don't know if your people have discovered this yet, but a pendulum," pointing to a long arm with a disc on the end, "always takes the same amount of time to swing– "

"Wait...what?"

"Let me show you." He went over to the corner and brought over something he had assembled earlier. It was a tripod with a light chain about 3 feet long hanging from the top. The chain had a solid metal ball attached to the bottom. After setting up the tripod, Scott gently pulled the ball to one side and let go. "Brandon, try timing the swings." Seeing Brandon looking at a timing candle he frowned and said, "Maybe use your heartbeat."

Brandon shrugged and putting a couple of his fingers on his wrist began to count quietly. He blinked. "It seems to be just about two beats per swing."

"Okay, now keep timing it." Scott pulled the ball back quite a bit further this time before letting go. After about a minute he stopped it, then pulled it a much shorter distance and let go again.

Brandon stopped counting after a little while and said slowly, "Wow, you're right. It always seems to take the same amount of time. Okay, how...." He looked back at the sketch. "Aha, because you know how long it's going to take to swing," he said, scratching his head. "Uh...go on."

Scott spread out the other paper. "Now, this is just an approximation because I've never actually built or even worked on one of these, and I only know the general principles, but here it is." He began to point out different parts. "The cord wraps around the shaft of this gear and the weight at the other end wants to fall, providing the power to turn it. This thing at the side is attached to the top of the pendulum. When the pendulum swings, this thing rocks back and forth...this other thing here only lets the gear turn one tooth at a time, while the other side kind of kicks the pendulum to keep it swinging. Since you know how fast the gear is going to move, you can set up the...uh... tooth count on these other connected gears so they move this pointer around the front of the clock to indicate time passing." He paused while Brandon examined the sketches. "Now since you use 100 beats per minute, and 50 minutes per mark, that will determine how many teeth go on which gear."

Brandon looked up. "This actually works? It looks very complicated!" He looked at the papers again. "It also seems to me that it's going to take incredibly fine craftsmanship to make all these things fit together."

Scott nodded. "Yes, it is kind of complex and it does

take skill." He rubbed his chin. "In my world some of the smaller ones have to be made by the same people who work on really fine jewelry." He sighed. "It may take a lot of testing and adjustments to get this right, but once they get all the sizes and tooth counts worked out, I expect they will be making quite a few of these before too long."

Brandon was still staring at the sketches. "If you say so. It seems like an awful lot of work instead of just lighting a candle"

Scott fought down mild annoyance. "I'm pretty sure your people will like these. And once they've worked out the basics and start making these, you'll wonder how you ever did without them."

CHAPTER
Eleven

MORGAN LOOKED AT THE SKETCHES THOUGHTFULLY, HIS MIND working. "Can you move these things while they are operating?"

Scott frowned. "Um...I...maybe. You'd have to be very gentle about it. Why?"

"I was thinking that you could start several of these at the same time, then put them in different places and...well, I can think of several uses for THAT!"

Scott smiled. "I can think of a better way. You set them up in different places then use 'telephone' or telecom pairs to start them at the same time."

Morgan snorted. "Yeah, I guess that would work too." He paused briefly. "Let me see if I can get some craftsmen to make some of these parts." He grumbled, "This won't be cheap, you know."

Scott said diffidently, "I was hoping that once the sizes

and everything are worked out, then the parts could be cast from molds."

The answer was a grunt as Morgan rolled up the sketches and swept out of the room.

Scott looked at Brandon. "Did he seem grumpier than usual to you?"

Brandon chuckled. "Maybe a little. I think Fredo has been very demanding lately. I get the impression that his brother-in-law isn't doing well again, and he gets stressed about living with his sister whenever that happens."

"Poor Fredo! Is his sister really THAT bad?"

Brandon frowned. "Well, I only met her once, very briefly, but yeah. Plus, there's some kind of family history there. I don't really know what."

"Huh, thanks."

Snapping his fingers, Brandon said, "I almost forgot. When we were talking about those gears and things earlier, you said something about little ones. How little can these clocks be and still work?"

Scott laughed. "Don't you remember the one I used to wear on my wrist?"

Brandon's eyes bugged out. "WHAT! That was a clock like this? Wait, that can't be. Where was the pendulum? How could you even fit– "

Scott held up his hand. "It isn't exactly the same, but it uses gears with teeth and an escapement just like the other, only smaller."

"What the heck is an escapement?"

"Oh, sorry, it's the thing you said looked like a claw, that only lets the wheel move one tooth at a time."

"Um…if there's no weight trying to fall, where does the power come from?"

Scott replied carefully, "You know what spring steel is, right?"

"Yeah, I think so. You bend it and it springs back to the way it was, right?"

"Yes, well, inside this is a long, thin piece of spring steel wound into a coil. The spring trying to unwind is what supplies the power."

Brandon sighed. "Okay, what happens when the spring has…uh…sprung back all the way? Wouldn't it just stop?"

Scott said, "Yes, with the older watches you had to retighten the spring every day or so. This one has some kind of arrangement inside that causes the spring to retighten a little when you move your arm."

"But…without the pendulum, how would the timing work?"

"As I understand it, there is some kind of deal with a flywheel and spring, the mainspring unwinds and pushes the flywheel until the other spring stops it, then the wheel…um…recoils and it starts again. If you know how heavy the wheel is and how strong the spring is, then you can figure out how fast that'll be."

"I'm not sure…" Brandon stopped abruptly when Scott stiffened and held up his hand, closing his eyes. Brandon waited somewhat apprehensively until Scott opened his eyes again. "Scott?"

Scott blinked rapidly. "Sorry about that. That was my Minthar friend. He said the captain is okay with transporting a small group of people between here and Land-below if necessary."

"Okay, what do they think of as 'a small group'?"

Scott shrugged. "He wasn't really specific. If I had to guess, maybe up to a dozen or so." He scratched his head. "Why don't we go tell Morgan, and then get something to eat?"

~⊃℃~

THINGS IN THE UNDERGROUND CITY OF LANDBELOW HAD improved lately. Some subtle shuffling of people under the guise of "restructuring the administration" had resulted in the people who had been identified as hostile being shifted to positions no longer having access to inside information. Since some of them had been actual promotions, Martin was reasonably sure that nobody was the wiser about the real reason. While he was still somewhat annoyed with Varney, *I still don't see why he would have a problem with asking a few people some questions,* he was pleased with the results. Sitting back in his chair, he looked at his friend and colleague, Winston. "So, how are the repairs at the entrance facility going?"

Winston frowned. "Well, we're making some progress. A couple of our people were able to follow what Scott had been doing well enough to fix a few of the problems. But I'm afraid that some things are still beyond us at the moment." He hesitated. "I am wondering about the advisability of asking Scott to return for a while to…give some advice?"

Martin drummed his fingers on the desk before answering slowly, "Even if the travel time wasn't prohibitive, I'm not sure I'm comfortable with that, at least at the moment. Have them keep trying for now." He thought for a few moments before continuing. "However, it might be wise to come up with a list of...topics for discussion, shall we say, should it prove necessary."

Winston brightened slightly. "Of course, I'll see to it."

"I know you will. In case I didn't tell you before, I am VERY glad you are back."

Winston rose to his feet. "Thank you, sir." He bowed slightly and left, closing the door behind him.

～⊃C～

IT WAS MORNING AND BRANDON HAD STOPPED BY TO HAVE breakfast with Scott and Morgan. "Hi, how is everybody this morning?"

Morgan's response was a laconic, "fine" as he concentrated on what he was reading.

Scott's growled, "Okay, I guess" caused Brandon to raise his eyebrows.

"Uh, Scott. Are you okay?"

Scott shook himself. "Yeah, sorry. I "talked" with my wife too long last night and I've got quite a headache."

"Oh...is everything alright?"

Scott sighed. "Well, to be honest, not really. I used to take the kids camping sometimes in the summer, and they are beginning to ask Lisa to do that, but it isn't really her thing, you know. After a while we sort of settled on a compromise that she get an RV. That way she can still be comfortable while Danny and Gwen have their choice of whether or not to actually use it. She was kind of okay with it, but wasn't sure about driving it. I tried to tell her that it probably wouldn't be all that different from driving the big van she uses sometimes for retreats, but she still seemed kind of nervous."

Brandon said carefully, "I'm sorry to hear that. I hope everything works out okay. Um, I don't understand...big van...RV?"

"Um...a big van is sort of like a long wagon that holds many people, and RV stands for Recreational Vehicle." Scott frowned. "Uh...picture one of those really long wagons complete with beds, a stove, a table, chairs, etc.... basically like a really tiny house on wheels."

"Huh! I can see where that could be hard to maneuver." Brandon hesitated. "You mention retreat, what would she be running away from?"

Scott roused enough to chuckle. "Oh, that. No, a retreat is...." He scratched his head. "Well, it's when she takes a yoga group to some quiet place, maybe in a small town so they can all talk and practice away from the people and things that might distract them. Maybe like when you go on a caravan, you don't have to worry about the problems around here while you're gone."

"Oh, okay."

Scott looked over at Morgan. "Sorry to bother you Morgan. Any news on the clock?"

Morgan looked up briefly. "Not yet. The little pieces are

almost done, then they'll have to assemble it. Might be a while." He went back to reading.

"Any more news from Varney?"

Morgan answered shortly, "No." Then suddenly said, "Wait." After reaching into a pocket in his cloak, he handed Scott a sealed message. "This was delivered earlier."

Scott broke the seal and opened the message.

Scott,

We heard from the village of S'Mark that they are going to hold an annual festival on the anniversary of the day their people were rescued from the "little monsters". They insist that you, Clem, Brandon and Geon be present, as well as anyone you care to invite. I got the impression that they are also planning some kind of sculpture or statue in your honor, no other details were supplied. I have taken the liberty of informing Clem and Geon. Would you kindly inform Brandon and ensure that both of you are available on that day?

Best wishes,
Wesley, Count of the town of Enimnori.

AFTER READING THE MESSAGE, SCOTT HANDED IT TO MORGAN, who read it and handed it back. "Make sure you tell Brandon. Oh, and just so you know, I think the new Baron is planning something as well. I have no idea what."

~ ꝯ ᴄ ~

SCOTT WOKE SUDDENLY TO THE SOUND OF LOUD CURSING. Quickly throwing on pants, he followed the noise to Morgan's workroom. As he approached, the cursing stopped to be replaced by shouting. "HOW DID THEY GET IN HERE?"

Entering the room somewhat cautiously, he immediately saw the reason for Morgan's anger. On the wall in the workroom, apparently written in blood, were the words *"THE DAY IS COMING"*. Morgan turned as he entered, clearly ready to scream at someone. He reined himself in slightly. "LOOK AT THIS!" He shook his fist and a trickle of dust fell from the ceiling as the room shook slightly. Stalking across the room, he dropped unceremoniously onto a stool, several of which could be seen lying in pieces on the other side of the room. He growled. "I'm gonna gut somebody for this!"

Scott said slowly. "I can understand sneaking past a few guards but I always assumed this place was magically guarded."

"IT IS!" Morgan snapped.

The rest of the day was spent with Morgan and several

other magicians trying to figure out what had happened, as well as several more guards milling around outside.

That evening when asked what had been discovered, Morgan replied, "All we are really sure of is that magic was used in the break in." He sighed. "We had several different possibilities, some using spells, some contained in magic items, but we haven't any way to tell which was used. Now I can defend against most of them, but I may have to have some more guards for a while."

Scott regarded Morgan thoughtfully. "I wonder if maybe that was the whole purpose of this."

Morgan sat back in his chair and sighed even more heavily. "I'm inclined to think the same thing. We certainly didn't get a lot done today, and this is going to be disruptive for a while, at least." He growled to himself. "The really annoying part is that even so we can't ignore it. We have to act as if it was a real threat. I ABSOLUTELY HATE THIS!"

Brandon said carefully, "I'm not sure I understand... you don't think someone is going to try something?"

Scott replied, "If you really want to hurt someone, steal things, etc., it seems kind of stupid to warn them first." He shrugged. "It does happen though, some people really are...uh...kind of off, if you know what I mean, and will do things the rest of us consider insane for reasons that seem good to them."

Brandon responded, "Uh, yeah, I guess I see. So what happens now?"

Morgan grumbled something under his breath, then said, "Well, I have a few more defenses to set up and then I will arrange for extra guards. Otherwise we will just continue as normal. Which reminds me. Scott, your clock is being assembled and tested. We should know in a week or so if it's going to work."

"Great! Fingers crossed."

Morgan continued, "And I think this would be a good time to start showing you how to defend against mind invasion."

Scott shuddered. "Yeah, that sounds like a good idea."

"Okay, to start with, reach out as if you were trying to connect with someone, but instead picture a barrier around yourself."

Scott focused. "Uh, like this?" He was startled by what felt like a pinprick behind his right eye. "I guess not."

"No, no, that was a start. There was resistance. Now as with a lot of magic, especially mind magic, everyone does it slightly differently. One of the things to remember is that an attack can take many forms. Some sharp like a mental arrow, some more like a falling rock, and some can be pretty subtle. The first step, of course, is to develop an awareness, which you already have. After that, most of us use a...." Morgan frowned. "Well, for me I picture something like a trench full of thick mud, so whatever is trying to get to me has to move slower and make noise."

Scott said slowly, "I think I understand. Give me a minute." After a few seconds of consideration, he pictured himself being surrounded by layer upon layer of thick, sticky string with several bells in it, imagining an incoming attack gathering more and more 'string' as it got closer, both slowing it down and blunting it. Nodding to Morgan, he waited. After a brief pause he 'heard' the bells ringing, then felt something like an invisible hand being stuck in the string briefly before withdrawing and his head began to ache.

Morgan's eyebrows shot up. "What did you do? Not only did I not get through, I felt like I was getting trapped!"

Scott described what he had done and asked, "You mean this headache isn't your doing?"

"Headache? No, that's just your mind reacting to the… uh…unaccustomed magic you used. It should bother you less and less the more you practice." He hesitated. "You may not need much else in the way of defense. If you can make this a bit stronger, it should be quite effective, although if it turns out to be too taxing, you may have to try something weaker and…um…farther away." Morgan smiled. "That was well done! Shockingly well done. Now, just practice until it becomes easy, and eventually you should be able to keep it up all the time without really thinking about it too much."

Scott responded, "Okay, I will, and thank you, both for the instruction and the compliment."

Morgan nodded, and looking pointedly at his desk, said gruffly, "Now go away. I have some work to do." Scott smiled and left.

⟋೨C⟍

IT DIDN'T TAKE TOO LONG FOR THINGS TO RETURN TO NORMAL (mostly), albeit with a few new subtle security measures and some not so subtle additions to the guard staff. It took over a week before the craftsmen were satisfied that Scott's clock design actually did work, and several more weeks of painstaking adjustments and experimentation before it started keeping time accurately. At first, the only people who could afford one were Morgan and Count Wesley, although Scott was sure that that would change once the word got out, and they were able to start mass producing the parts that now had to be painstakingly made by hand.

As predicted, Brandon's skepticism evaporated very quickly after only a couple of experiments in Morgan's lab.

Scott smirked at Brandon. "Are you sure you wouldn't rather just light a candle?"

Brandon smiled back. "Alright already. I freely admit that this new clock, invented through the inestimable genius of the famous Sir Scott, Hero of Enimnori, is very useful." He bowed low. "Forgive me for having doubted you, oh Great One!"

Scott bowed back. "Why, thank you. Coming from the great Brandon, Hero of Enimnori and noted preserver of fish eggs; that is a compliment indeed."

Morgan snapped. "If you two are QUITE finished, can we please get back to work?"

The two of them exchanged glances, then bowed simultaneously saying loudly, "Yes Master!" actually causing Morgan to laugh and drop the notebook he had been holding. Sighing, he picked it up and glaring at them both said, "Well Scott, congratulations. This last improvement to your telephone devices is working even better than we hoped. They are a bit smaller, a little easier to make and still have the same range! Excellent."

"Well, honestly, a couple of the improvements were Brandon's idea, so I will have to share the credit."

"Well, good job to both of you. Now go away, I have some vineyard business to attend to."

Brandon spoke first. "I wouldn't mind a snack and maybe a mug of beer. What do you say Scott?"

"I say...let's do it! Hillview Tavern?"

"Hillview Tavern!"

They both turned to leave.

～つC～

THEY RETURNED TO FIND AN ANGRY MORGAN PACING BACK and forth in his study while holding a crumpled piece of paper.

After watching him for a moment, Scott carefully cleared his throat. "Uh...Morgan, what's up?"

Morgan dropped heavily into his chair. "It's my brother. He can't simply put some extra security measures in place. Oh no, not Harold. He just has to know everything that's going on. NOW he wants to help. SURE he does, he just wants to be 'in the know' and be able to hint and wink about it. Huh." He scowled at both of them. "So now he is coming here tomorrow, and I have to drop whatever I am doing to fill him in! After all, it's not like I could possibly be doing something important, right?"

Brandon said carefully, "Well, he is kind of an important person, so wouldn't he be able to...uh...I don't know, help with getting stuff from the Count or the new Baron maybe?"

Morgan huffed impatiently. "I suppose so. It's just the self important tone that always makes me crazy. He can't just do something quietly. He just has to make a big deal out of it, with messengers running back and forth and cloaked figures arriving in carriages." Waving the paper, he added. "So now, I have to reply by special messenger tonight so his highness, the ambassador can come with his entourage tomorrow."

Scott said slowly, "Isn't it a bad idea to spread this all around? I would think he would want to keep it quiet?"

Morgan snorted. "Oh, don't worry. Everybody he brings will have to wait outside so as to keep the secret. He isn't stupid. He just has to make a big production out of it. Oh well, I'll have to write a response, and let my people know that we will be having guests tomorrow."

The next afternoon, as Morgan had predicted, a coach accompanied by ten guardsmen in full uniform pulled up, and a distinguished looking gentleman was ushered into the study. Morgan smiled slightly, extending his hand. "Harold."

The other man took the offered hand. "Morgan." Turning his head, he nodded to the other two in the room. "I remember Brandon. Congratulations on your many contributions to Enimnori. You are indeed a brave and worthy fellow." Shaking Brandon's hand briefly he then turned to Scott. "And this is the famous and mysterious Sir Scott. It is indeed a pleasure to finally make your acquaintance." He again extended his hand. "I have heard so much about you, and I finally get to meet you. I cannot tell you what an honor this is."

Scott shook the offered hand and responded warily, "Thank you. You are too kind."

"Not at all. Not at all." Turning back to his brother, he said graciously, "Perhaps we could all be seated? We have several things to discuss." At a gesture from Morgan, they all sat down. "I understand that we have you two to thank for the return of those missing villagers a while back, although I must admit that the reports were somewhat vague about the circumstances. Would you fill me in please?" After a somewhat abbreviated explanation, he said slowly, "Now I see why the reports were vague. Morgan, I'll be honest. If this was coming from someone else, I would be disinclined to believe it." His brow furrowed. "You and Wesley were right to keep this under wraps. I think the general population might have serious difficulty dealing with this. So, if I understand correctly, these…creatures were offered some kind of mining rights in exchange for not enslaving us?"

Morgan nodded. "That is essentially correct. It seems that both of our moons are very high in valuable minerals."

Harold actually chuckled. "So you bribed them with the rights to something that we can't use anyway? I am very impressed."

After sharing a look with Morgan, Scott said carefully, "It wasn't our idea actually. It was the other aliens who came up with it."

There was a very brief silence. "Other aliens? You mean

those mysterious allies spoken of are ALSO not from our world? Why are these creatures showing up here?"

Morgan replied, "We honestly have no idea. Our allies mentioned some kind of distress call. But we certainly didn't send one, and according to Varney the people in Landbelow knew nothing about any of this."

"How can we be sure of...oh...of course. I assume that this Varney is another magician?"

"That's correct."

"Yes, I think I remember him. Grey hair, very intelligent, doesn't talk much?"

"Yes, that's him."

"An excellent choice." Turning his attention to Scott once more, he went on, "Now I understand we also have you to thank for the devices that let us stay in contact with our new allies near Dead Lake?"

Scott nodded. "Partly, although Morgan did a lot of the work and Brandon was instrumental in the testing."

"You are very modest, sir. However, it was your idea was it not?"

"Yes."

He regarded Scott thoughtfully. "I think we all owe you a great deal." He sat quietly for a moment, then seemed to come to a decision. Leaning forward he spoke directly to Scott. "I hope you will consider me a friend and ally. Please feel free to call on me for assistance at any time. I know some of my colleagues can be...difficult at times. You are invited to use my name if needed." He held up a hand as Morgan started to speak. "I know the family took a dim view of your chosen profession and abilities

Morgan, and I want to let you know that even if their opinions have not changed, mine have. I must be taking my leave soon. I have to travel to the capital soon to brief the king." He winked. "Any more special packages for Fredo's brother-in-law?"

Morgan rolled his eyes. "Yeah, I'll make up a few 'healing potions' for you to take. Thanks."

"No problem." He turned. "It was nice to see you again Brandon, and I hope to see you soon, Sir Scott."

Scott took the proffered hand. "Just Scott will do. It was nice meeting you as well."

After he had left, they sat in silence for several minutes. Finally, Morgan cleared his throat. "Ahem, ah, that went quite differently than expected."

Scott said. "Do you think he was serious about helping and all that?"

Morgan seemed to have difficulty speaking. "Yes. Yes he was," he responded slowly.

CHAPTER

Twelve

SEBULAN MAKARA WAS SMILING. "SO THAT LITTLE DEVICE OUR magician friend Jons made for you actually worked?"

The man known as Stumpy (but only behind his back if you wanted to live) replied, "Yes it did." He smirked. "We left the message on the wall, painted in blood, and got out with no one the wiser. They ain't NEVER gonna figure out how either!" He stretched lazily in the chair in front of Makara's desk. "It was real funny watching them runnin' around like crazy people. Now they got themselves some extra guards, and it wouldn't surprise me none if they was wettin' themselves nights wonderin' what's gonna happen next! It was almost worth doin' the job just to see the looks on their faces."

"I'm pleased that you are so happy. So does that mean I don't have to pay you?" Makara said sarcastically.

"Nah, wouldn't want the word gettin' around. Might be bad fer business, ya know?"

A snort, "Yeah, I get it. Here you are." He passed over a small bag. "It was worth it. Now were you able to plant that thing that Jons said would let us hear them?"

"Well, I stuck it under one of the benches but near's I can tell, it don't work."

"That's okay. I would have been surprised if it did. Morgan may be a simpering pile of garbage, but he is a magician after all." He sighed. "It would have been nice, but oh well. And how about Ronn's plans?"

The man grimaced. "They're goin' too slow fer my taste. We got a couple of guys training with those rifle things, but it ain't as easy as it looks. Especially when you can hardly see the target 'cause it's so far away."

"And the other part?" Makara asked somewhat impatiently.

"Not so good right now. They don't need any new trackers so he couldn't get in. But who knows, trackin's real dangerous, if you get my meanin'," Stumpy smirked unpleasantly.

Makara snapped, "No accidents! That might make them suspicious! Just stick with the plan!" He paused. "Now if Morgan happened to have an accident now...." He reached into a drawer and pulled out a larger bag of coins, jingling it suggestively.

Stumpy licked his lips, then shrugged. "I'll think on it but the coward is always either at the vineyard, his house, or at the castle with witnesses hangin' all over him." He glanced at the bag again and repeated slowly, "I'll think on it." He turned and left.

Makara hefted the bag thoughtfully before returning

it to the drawer. *That pile of crap Morgan has a lot to answer for.* Not only had Morgan's testimony gotten him arrested and jailed years ago, but his stump still ached where he had lost part of his leg during a failed attack on the castle that Morgan was helping defend. *Perhaps if his little toady Brandon was to die during a caravan raid,* he thought wistfully. He sighed. *No, It's probably better that they stay up nights worrying...perhaps if Morgan's house caught on fire....*

⁓つC⁓

SCOTT TAPPED BRANDON ON THE SHOULDER. "THIS BUSINESS with the writing on the wall," he said, chuckling to himself, "reminded me of something else."

Brandon looked at him. "Why do you always smile or laugh when you talk about the writing on the wall? What's funny about it?"

Smiling slightly, Scott said, "Sorry it's a literary reference from my world. It would take too long to explain. Maybe some other time." He took a breath. "Anyway, what I was wondering is, could you enchant a shirt or gambeson or something so that when it gets hit the impact gets spread out?"

Brandon frowned slightly. "I'm not sure what you mean by 'spread out'?"

Scott thought for a moment, then poked Brandon, first with his index finger, then with the flat of his hand.

"Oh! Umm, yeah I think so...." Brandon's eyebrows went up. "I GET IT! Yes, that way an arrow or bolt wouldn't go in, it would just bounce off!" he said excitedly.

Scott clapped him on the shoulder. "Exactly! It would still hurt a lot, and might even knock you down. But that's a whole lot better than having it sticking out of you."

With a laugh, Brandon replied, "Yeah, I can see that." He steepled his fingers and frowned, his eyes going distant. "Hmmmm, I...may have to think about this for a while."

"Okay, I think I'm in the mood for some fresh fruit. Do you want some too?"

"Uh...sure, please."

Smiling, Scott headed for the door. As he left, he cast the emotional awareness spell, happy that it had finally become a habit. Glancing around he detected the expected awareness mixed with worry from the guards stationed carefully in the shadows (which increased slightly as they realized he was leaving). As his two personal guards fell in step with him he suddenly became aware that the guard by the side door was feeling exceptional calm. Turning his head slightly, he saw nothing unusual until he finally realized that the guard seemed to be concentrating more on the sky than on the house he was supposedly guarding. He stopped suddenly, patting his pockets before saying, "Crap! Wait here, I'll be back in a minute," and went back inside. Walking quickly to the study he sat down, and closing his eyes, focused on his crystal and reached out with his mind...*Morgan, we may have a small problem.*

<surprise>I must say you are getting better at this! What's wrong?

As I was leaving the house, I noticed that one of the guards seems VERY interested in the clouds and seems especially calm. It may be nothing, but....

<concern>I see your point. Concentrate for a moment on which guard it was...okay, I see it. I will check into this and let you know. <pride>Nice job, you are really coming along!

After getting back with the fruit, Scott went directly to the workroom. He saw Brandon sitting on one of the new stools somewhat dejectedly playing with a knife. On the bench next to him was a heavy linen shirt with several holes in it. "What's with the knife?"

Brandon shrugged. "It was easier than trying to set up something with a crossbow, and it's kind of the same thing, right?"

Scott thought about it. "Well, in some ways yes, in some ways no."

"What do you mean?"

"Ah, first, I don't think it would be as fast as an arrow or bolt. Second, it's under power, not just flying through the air. I don't really know what kind of difference that makes to what you are trying to do, but they are differences."

Brandon scratched his head. "I don't see where...." He sighed. "Never mind. Will you help me find and test with a small crossbow, then?"

"Oh, sure. Why don't we take a short trip to the armory and see what they've got that we can borrow." Brandon nodded, and they headed for the door.

Scott hesitated as they were about to go out. "I forgot to tell you, but earlier one of the guards outside seemed to be focused more on the clouds than on the house, if you get my drift. Don't be obvious about it, but check as we leave and tell me if you sense anything odd. Oh, Morgan knows already. I told him earlier."

Brandon blinked. "When was Morgan here?"

"He wasn't." Scott tapped his head suggestively.

'Huh? Oh...I forgot you could do that....I still can't, not really." Brandon said woefully.

Scott snorted. "And I can't lift or move nearly as much as you can. Everybody's different. I kind of suck at telling the weather too."

Brandon seemed to cheer up a little at hearing this. "Okay...alright, spell's cast. Let's go get us a crossbow."

After leaving the vicinity of Morgan's house, Scott said quietly, "I didn't notice anything unusual this time. Did you?"

Brandon shook his head. "Nope, I didn't either. I'll be sure to check when I go in and out, though."

A couple of minutes later after stopping at a fruit vendor, Scott said quietly, "I think we're being followed. I want to try something. You stay here and pick out some nice fruit. I'm going to go way over to the other side of the square to buy a new shirt and see if he or she follows me. I shouldn't be too long."

Brandon smiled, and, pointing to some of his favorite fruit, said, "Got it! I'll be right here," while carefully going through the baskets as if looking for the best pieces.

Smiling, Scott proceeded to cross the busy square while trying to concentrate on the 'mental signature' he had been aware of since soon after they left Morgan's.

After purchasing a new shirt, he proceeded to walk around, stopping at several other vendors along the way. Finally returning to the fruit vendor he asked Barndon if he had had any luck.

"Yep! Got some great fruit here." He paid for the fruit, then hesitating, asked, "Where to next?"

Scott shrugged. "We might as well do what we came for." He smirked. "I think maybe we should stop by the far edge of the vineyard on the way back, though. Just to see how things are going." He winked at Brandon who chuckled.

Arriving back at the workroom a couple of hours later carrying a light crossbow, a case of bolts, and several cheap linen shirts, Brandon chuckled and said, "I wonder if our watcher has sore feet now?" He sat down heavily. "I know mine are a little tired. That was brilliant, by the way, arguing about those shirts and going back to the market twice!"

Scott laughed. "Why, thank you. I thought it was a nice touch. I thought I was sensing tiredness and frustration, and just wanted to 'help out' a bit." He carefully set the crossbow on one of the workbenches and went looking for something to clamp it down with while Brandon set up a large melon on another table across the room.

Brandon laughed again. "I like the idea of using melons for targets too. If there's anything left, we can have a snack later!"

That got him a look. "Your stomach is very important to you, isn't it Brandon?"

"Yeah, I guess so." He finished by putting one of the

new shirts on the melon in question. He then stood back, and consulting his notes carefully, cast a spell on the shirt. "Okay...ready."

Scott pulled the trigger...THOCK...The bolt penetrated most of its length into the melon. Sighing, Brandon consulted his notes again, cast another spell and nodded to Scott. THOCK! A few minutes later...THOCK! After several more attempts with the same result, Brandon sat down heavily. "Crap! That was my last idea."

Scott said slowly, "I wonder if you could key off the pressure wave instead of the bolt itself? Maybe that would help."

Brandon stared at him blankly. "Key off the pressure...." His face cleared, and his eyes lit up. He spent several minutes alternatively writing in his notebook and staring into space mumbling to himself, his eyes distant while Scott waited patiently. Finally, he took a deep breath and, getting a new shirt, cast a spell on it before 'dressing' the melon. "Okay...ready!"

Scott pulled the trigger...THOCK...Brandon looked crestfallen, but Scott hurried over and, looking closely, exclaimed, "YES! I thought it sounded different. It went in only about half as far! You're definitely on the right track!"

Confidence restored, Brandon spent several more minutes scanning his notes. On the next try, the bolt barely penetrated at all. Less than a mark later, they had the satisfaction of seeing a bolt bounce off and fall to the floor. Brandon said, "Well it didn't go through but it still made a big mushy spot."

Scott said cheerfully, "If that was a person, he would be

bruised but alive. That is GREAT Brandon! Now if you can make a couple for each of us, and Morgan too, I'll feel a bit safer."

Brandon looked at him. "Um…I thought you knew, this will only last a day or two, three at the most. I haven't mastered permanent enchantments yet."

Now it was Scott's turn to look crestfallen. "Well, um… that's still better than nothing." He regarded the shirt thoughtfully. "How hard is it to cast, and can you show me how?"

Brandon hesitated. "Um…well, it is kind of draining. I'm not sure if it would work for you. Why don't we try tomorrow. I'm kind of wiped out."

"Oh, sure. Sorry about the misunderstanding."

"Okay, no problem. Then once Morgan gets some free time, maybe he can help us."

Morgan looked up from his paperwork. "I'm sorry. I'm caught up now. What was it you two wanted to try?" After hearing Scott's explanation, he frowned. "I don't think you can do that to something after it's been made. Permanent things almost always have to be created that way. Like the invisible light detector, the magic had to be done as it was made; not after."

Scott was disappointed. "Oh. Okay, sorry to bother you." He paused for a moment. "So one of us would have to learn how to make a shirt, and cast spells while you were making it? Do you think I could learn how to do that?"

After regarding him thoughtfully and reading Brandon's notes again, Morgan said carefully, "There is honestly no way of knowing until you try. Creating permanent magic seems to be one of those things you have to be born with. It wouldn't take me more than a day or two to teach you how to make something simple. Then we'll know if it's at least possible." He smiled at Brandon. "You may not remember, but I had you try this once during your student days, and as it turns out, you unfortunately don't have the talent." Seeing Brandon's face, he hastened to add, "Most magicians don't have it either, so it's nothing to feel bad about." He snapped his fingers. "Oh, and before I forget, you will both be interested to know that there have been a few schedule changes among the guard staff."

Toward the end of the second day, Morgan sighed and said quietly to Scott, "Well, it seems that you don't have the ability to create permanent magic. Now, as I told Brandon, this is nothing to be ashamed of. It's inborn and very few have it. I'm only aware of five in recent years; two are dead, one disappeared years ago, leaving just two…Valtir and I."

Scott blinked. "Is that why Wesley never wants to let you go anywhere?"

Morgan said sourly, "Yeah, that's a piece of it." He shrugged. "Although to be honest, we've known each other a LONG time, so part of it is just him trying to protect a friend."

"He does seem like a decent guy." Frowning, Scott continued, "I had hopes for a while about lightweight protection, but I can't see someone recasting spells every couple of days just on the off chance somebody might get shot at." Scott shrugged. "Oh, well. So, what's the story about the guy who disappeared? Was he in a caravan that got ambushed or something?"

"Hardly! He was accused of molesting some students but disappeared just before he was going to be arrested."

"Huh! I see. Hey, wait. There had to be a magician helping Makara when he was trying to brainwash Brandon. Do you suppose...."

Morgan scowled. "Yes, I always thought it might be him, but since it doesn't really matter...." He spread his hands.

"I was just wondering if there was anything about his...uh...style I guess you would say that could help against him?"

"No, sorry. We weren't that close. He was an apprentice of Mohrs, not me. And Mohrs died a while ago."

"Um, how did he die?"

Morgan shrugged. "He was 96."

Scott grimaced. "Oh. Sorry. I must be getting paranoid."

"No need to be sorry. Trust me, if it had looked like anything but natural causes, we would have looked at Jons first." He paused. "Scott, your people must use some kind of lightweight protection, or you wouldn't have asked. How do they do it?"

"I'm not really sure. I think it has something to do with special fibers, interwoven somehow." He paused, brow furrowing. "I think that something called Kevlar is used a lot, but all I know is that it is some kind of advanced plastic compound."

"Plastic?" Morgan raised his eyebrows at the English word.

'Yeah, that's kind of a general name for a class of materials made by...by...." He paused, searching his memory. "All I know is that they are made by forcing molecules to join together in long chains, and that they can have very different properties depending on the materials and the process. Honestly I never understood it all that well," he finished almost plaintively.

Morgan forced himself not to smile or laugh. *Wow! Scott REALLY hates not knowing something.* He said carefully. "Don't worry about it."

Smiling weakly, Scott turned and left.

Sometime later, Scott, Brandon and Geon were eating at the Hillview Tavern. Setting down his spoon, Geon said quietly, "So it's been a while since we had a chance to talk. What's new?"

Brandon said cheerfully, "Scott's newest invention is a success! We can now make a machine that will keep track of time."

"I remember you guys talking about that. I'm glad it works." Geon hesitated before going on. "I don't think I'm supposed to know this, but I overheard something about an attack at Master Morgan's home?"

Glancing around quickly, Brandon answered very quietly, "Someone got into Morgan's house and wrote 'the day is coming' in blood on the wall of his workroom. They also...." he stopped as Scott suddenly made a sharp gesture with his hand.

Brandon's eyes flickered from side to side. He sucked

in his breath sharply. "If you will excuse me," he said in a conversational tone. "I have to use the restroom. I won't be long." Rising quickly to his feet he headed for the back of the tavern.

Geon looked at Scott and raised his eyebrows. "What just happened?"

Scott answered almost under his breath, "Someone is paying very close attention to our conversation. We're going to try and...DAMN IT!" He rose to his feet smoothly and turned barely in time to catch a fleeting glimpse of a figure hurrying out the door. "Crap! Come on! Maybe we can still catch her." He started for the door, only to almost trip over one of the servers hurrying past. After untangling himself and apologizing, he sighed and reseated himself, saying, "Sorry, maybe next time," as Brandon came back into the room. The guards who had also risen to their feet, ostentatiously walked over to the bar to ask for more bread, before also reseating themselves.

Geon hesitated, then said slowly, "I probably should also mention that there are rumors going around that you two drink too much. Now, I know that you don't, but some people, well, you know how it is, they just like to spread gossip." He spread his hands helplessly.

Scott felt himself getting angry. "And, how long has this been going on?"

Geon looked uncomfortable. "Maybe a couple of weeks."

Seeing Scott's face, Brandon said, "We don't drink too much! Why would people say that?" He shrugged. "Who cares, anyway. There's always a lot of talk going around and nobody really pays attention to it...do they?"

"Well, sometimes if the same thing gets repeated over and over again, people start to think that since they've heard this so many times, then hey, maybe it IS true." Scott scowled. "I've seen people's lives ruined over rumors like this." He sighed. "The worst thing is, that a lot of the time if you try and point out that it isn't true, you end up sounding defensive, you know, like you're hiding something. But if you DON'T say anything those same people think, 'if it isn't true, then why doesn't he just say so?' So you're screwed either way." Grinding his teeth, he went on, "Just try and keep track of where you hear these things, and keep us updated, if you don't mind."

Geon looked shocked. "Um...sure." Glancing at a shadow on the floor he said, "I should get going. Talk to you guys later."

CHAPTER
Thirteen

"So here's the plan," Ronn Tracker said. The explanation took several minutes. At the end he added, "We've already started, and the beauty of this is, that there's absolutely nothing they can do about it!"

Sebulon Makara found himself smiling. "I like it. You don't think it can be traced back to us?"

"I don't see how, and it probably doesn't matter anyway." He grinned. "If the second part works, then they REALLY look like fools, but if it doesn't and they make a fuss about it, they'll sound crazy." He laced his fingers together behind his head and leaned back in the chair.

Makara hesitated, then reached into his desk and hefted a small sack of coins. Handing it across the desk, he smiled again and said, "I think this deserves a bonus."

Bowing his head graciously, Ronn took the bag. "I am happy to help." Hefting the bag, he grinned, "In more ways than one."

~つC~

It was early evening and Scott was relaxing on a hillside overlooking part of Morgan's vineyard. He had previously made a promise to 'call' his wife briefly, and realized that this was as good a time as any. "Hey, John?"

"Yes s...uum. Yeah, Scott?"

"Can you guys please make sure I'm not distracted for a few minutes? I'm going to...um...." He paused, not sure of how to explain what he was about to do.

John looked uncomfortable, having been told several times by various people that he did NOT want to know what Scott was really doing most of the time. "That's okay, I really don't need to know...we'll just keep watch from... over there." He said hastily, pointing to a tree about 20 feet away. "Come on, Karg." The two guards moved off.

Scott chuckled. "Okay, guys. Thanks. I shouldn't be too long." He leaned back against a convenient large rock, closed his eyes and focused on wanting to talk to his wife. He was at first startled when nothing seemed to happen, then realized that his mental protection was still active. *It is getting so much easier to do that, Morgan was right. Practice makes perfect,* he thought happily. He carefully envisioned the phantom barrier of tangled gluey string extending around the picket fence through which he 'spoke' to his wife. *Lisa? Lisa?* He repeated the call several times and was just about to give up and try later, when the image of his smiling wife appeared. *Sorry, my love. I was on the phone.*

Anything wrong?

No, not at all. I was just setting up some arrangements with my staff.

Oh?

Yes. Scott, the kids REALLY want to go camping. Now that school is out they have more free time and, well, it was something they used to do with you and they seemed to think it would help. I didn't want to at first, but then after I practiced driving the RV like you suggested, I felt better about it, and I realized that that might be a good time to tell them, you know about us talking, and you being okay?

I suppose it would be better to tell them when you are all off by yourselves.

I think so too. It has been hard keeping this from them for so long. Do you think you could talk to them, too?

I'm not really sure. I don't think they are as open to this kind of thing as you were, especially Gwen. Once you are all alone, I can try. Let me know and I will make sure not to be busy for a while. How long a trip are you planning?

I was thinking of taking them up to the mountains for three or four days. Since weekends tend to be busy, I figure we would leave Monday afternoon and come back late Friday.

That should be fine. I can stay in the house and work on some things with Brandon so I will be available.

You really like this Brandon, don't you?

Yes, I think you would too…he reminds me a little bit of Danny. I wish I could meet him.

Maybe someday…who knows.

I was making arrangements for the week after next, will that be okay?

That should be fine. I have some things I wanted to try out that would be best done behind closed doors anyway.

It isn't dangerous, is it?

<chuckle> No, at least not for me.

<worry> What do you mean?

Well, just for fun, I have been thinking of a few different ways to protect myself, should the need arise.

Are you in danger?

Not really, well, no more than usual. I'm just trying to be prepared. You know how I am, 'suspenders and belt'.

<sigh> Yes, I know. I should make a couple of more calls, now that I know the timing will be okay. I love you.

I love you, too, honey.

Stretching, Scott started to stand up. Just as he noticed both of his guards slumped against the nearby tree, he felt his mental alarm going off. Strengthening his defense, he looked around quickly to see several people approaching. Oddly they didn't seem to be armed except for three of them holding small tubes. *Those look like really short blow-pipes,* he thought, then realized that they must be the source of the mental attack. Remembering how Brandon had told about being sleepy all the time while he was being held captive, and seeing that his guards seemed unharmed, he forced himself to yawn, and then slump forward slightly. Gratifyingly, two of them put away the tubes, and taking out half full wineskins, began to dribble wine liberally over his two guards, before placing the now nearly empty skins on the ground, one next to each of them. One of them pulled out another half empty wineskin and began to walk toward the seemingly unconscious Scott.

Since it seemed that they weren't about to kill him, he waited until the man got quite close before reacting visibly. He mentally pictured a large wooden mallet striking the rearmost man in the head as he poured power into it, and surprisingly the man staggered and collapsed. The others stopped in confusion. The woman in front pointing the tube at him and blowing into it, shock evident on her face when instead of collapsing, he rose to his feet and swung the staff, knocking her legs out from under her. She fell, but rolled gracefully out of reach and springing to her feet began running, yelling to her comrades to grab the fallen one and follow her. Scott quickly jabbed the closest one with his staff. The man convulsed and dropped to the ground, twitching slightly. One of the others charged, grabbed the staff, nearly wrenching it away from him before Scott swept his legs out from under him. Unlike the woman, he dropped heavily to the ground. Scott spun, and with a quick blow knocked him unconscious. The others scattered and ran off. Scott let them go and carefully watching the three on the ground, went to check on his guards. Both were breathing normally, and a relieved Scott focused through a growing headache and sent out a mental call for Brandon.

The interrogation of the attackers was not very fruitful. The woman who had escaped was the leader, and the others knew only the part that they had been hired to do. The only good news was that they had gotten ahold of one of the 'blowguns' that put people to sleep.

Morgan fingered the 'blowgun' carefully. "Well, this is most likely Jons' work, and, as much as I despise him personally, this is beautifully done. It is compact, sturdy and made out of commonly obtainable, inexpensive materials." He sighed heavily. "What a waste. He could have gone far if he had been able to keep himself in check. Now he works with criminals and madmen." Setting the device down he said brusquely, "Our testing yesterday shows that it is effective to a range of about 30 feet. Our test subjects remained asleep for four to five marks unless disturbed, and were VERY difficult to wake up for the first mark or so." Turning to Armis, he said, "Please convey my thanks to all those guardsmen and hunters who volunteered. Having so many volunteers willing to be tested made this go a lot faster."

Armis chuckled. "Well, you had made it clear that it was just something that put people to sleep, so a lot of them considered it just a way of getting some rest while still being paid for it. But, I will pass along your thanks. Now do you think you can come up with a way to defend against this? Quite frankly, I find the...implications of this disturbing. I can imagine all kinds of things I could do with something like this." Pausing to take a sip of water, he continued, "I got the impression just now that it would be cheap and easy to make more of these. How much do I need to be worried about these things?"

Morgan responded slowly, "I wouldn't call it exactly easy. Don't forget he has to make them all personally." He stroked his beard absently. "I would estimate it would take a couple of days of pretty intense focus to make this, and it might be weeks before he could make another one. This kind of thing is pretty draining even if you have someone to supply some...uh...help," he said, smiling fondly at Brandon. "So I wouldn't worry about dozens of them showing up. In fact, it wouldn't surprise me if those were all he had. I don't remember him as being particularly industrious or hard working." He scowled. "I expect he is charging his employer a small fortune for these things though."

Armis relaxed somewhat. "What about defending against them?"

Morgan pondered this before replying. "I will have to test a few things, but I don't think there will be too much I can do to protect a non-magician from these, and even if I can come up with something, it may end up taking too much time, or be too expensive." Frowning thoughtfully, he went on, "I will try, however, and might be able to come up with something."

Armis turned to Scott. "What about you? What do you think? You managed to protect yourself, would you be able to do that for somebody else?"

Scott looked unhappy. "I'm afraid I'm too new at this to know. I will try, though."

Morgan spoke up. "It is possible, in fact likely that Scott would be able to protect someone close to him to a certain extent, but it will take a while to figure it out. Sorry."

Armis sighed. "Oh well, at least we have an idea about what to watch out for. Keep me posted and I will quietly pass it along." He rose to his feet and left.

Scott cleared his throat. "Ah...Brandon, if you don't

mind my asking, is that bracelet you gave to Marta the other day rare, or expensive?"

Brandon looked surprised. "No, not– " He stopped as someone knocked on the door.

Morgan called out. "Yes? Come in."

The door opened to reveal a somewhat dirty and disheveled young man. "Sorry to bother you, Uncle Morgan. I just wanted to let you know that those new roses have been planted."

Morgan smiled. "Thank you, Don. I appreciate it. Are any of the others still here?"

"Just Mary, these others wanted to get home early. Momma is making biscuits, and there's always a big fight over who gets to taste them first."

Morgan laughed at that. "Yes, I am WELL aware of the quality of your mother's cooking. Especially her biscuits." He patted his stomach and winked. The young man chuckled and left, closing the door behind him.

Scott found himself smiling. "Uncle Morgan?"

Morgan, still smiling slightly, said. "He's one of Fredo's grandchildren. I've been 'Uncle Morgan' for decades now. I kind of like it actually."

Scott said wistfully, "He's about my son's age." There was a brief moment of silence before he shook himself. "Anyway, Brandon, I have a modification I want to try on my staff, and I could use some copper, so I was wondering if it's rare or expensive."

Brandon scratched his chin. "No, not really, what do you need it for?"

Scott replied, "Well, somebody tried to grab my staff

during the...uh...hillside incident, and it got me thinking. If I run a couple of thin strips of copper along the sides then I could just let go of it and let them zap themselves."

Brandon burst out laughing. "That would be fitting justice, wouldn't it! Why copper though?"

Scott smiled. "I just need a good conductor. Gold would be best, but I really don't want to run around carrying a staff with gold on it."

"Yeah, I see your point. Shouldn't be too hard to get some."

It took less than a day to obtain the copper needed and Scott was able to quickly 'decorate' his staff.

Brandon smiled. "You know, I think I may make myself a staff. That looks really neat." He looked thoughtful. "Could you show me how to fight with it if I do?"

Scott smiled back. "Why, thank you. And, yes I can give you some tips. I also have something else to show you." He frowned. "I keep forgetting to ask, is there any kind of rule against attacking somebody with magic...even if you are defending yourself?"

"No. At least not that I am aware of. Why?"

"Just wanted to make sure. Here...watch this." Scott took a lead musket ball out of his pouch, and with a flick of his wrist sent it flying across the room. There was a sharp crack as it bounced off the opposite wall hard enough to leave a small dent in the wood. "It just takes a little magic to speed it up and aim it."

Brandon blinked, walked over and picked up the ball before returning to the other side of the room. Focusing on it, he tried the same thing, only to have it impact low on the ceiling. He tried several more times with similar results. He sighed. "I can throw it, but it doesn't hit where I want it to." He tried again, this time smashing a small mug quite a distance away from where he had been aiming. "Ugh, I think I see why nobody does this. You seem to have a talent for making things do what you want." He tossed the little ball back to Scott who put it back in his pouch.

"Thanks. Here's something else I was going to show you," he said, pulling out a set of three cords, fastened at the center with lead weights attached to the ends. "My people call this a bola. I can't demonstrate in here 'cause it takes too much room. You swing it around your head and throw it at somebody, or some critter. If you do it right, it tangles their legs and they fall down." Stuffing it back into a bag, he went on, "I plan on having the guards carry them whenever we go outside the city. What do you think?"

Brandon scratched his head. "Interesting, I guess. I wonder what the guards will think?"

Scott shrugged. "I guess I'll find out later. When are those guys coming over to help test the sleep tube?"

Glancing at the large grandfather clock now decorating the corner of the workshop, Brandon said slowly, "I think they said midafternoon, so it should be soon." Seeing Scott smiling, he sighed and said resignedly, "Yes, I like the new clock. Yes, it's very handy to have around, and no I wouldn't rather just light a candle."

"I didn't say a word...AH! I guess they're here early," Scott replied as there came a knocking at the door.

About a mark later, looking at nine snoring guardsmen

scattered around the room, Scott said dejectedly, "Well, THAT didn't work so well. It didn't even work when I was standing right next to them." He looked at the last conscious guard. "Do you mind hanging around and waking them up in a mark or so?"

The man laughed. "Absolutely, sir!"

Scott smiled back. "Sorry to stick you with such a nasty job, but we don't want them here all night. Thanks."

"The man smiled and pulled a stool into a comfortable position. Glancing somewhat uncomfortably at the large clock, he said, "You don't mind if I use a candle do you?"

"No, that's fine."

Later at supper, Scott said to Brandon, "My wife wants me to try and communicate with the children tonight. I may need your help. Do you mind?"

"Of course not."

After chatting for a while, they both arose and went to Morgan's study, where they seated themselves. *Morgan was right, this is much more comfortable than the workroom.* Scott thought. *It was nice of him to suggest it.*

Brandon settled into his chair. It had been decided that he would help only if Scott asked, or if it looked like he was weakening.

Scott settled himself, focused and mentally called his wife. *Lisa…Lisa?*

I'm here!

Are the kids with you?

Danny is here. When I tried to explain, Gwen said that I was crazy, and that she wanted nothing to do with this. I'm sorry, I tried.

Don't be sorry. Gwen is right, this DOES sound crazy. Let me see if I can sense Danny at all... Focusing, and drawing power from his crystal, Scott could dimly see a figure near his wife. He tried calling his son's name, and thought he saw the figure turn toward him. Gesturing to Brandon, he funneled even more power into his attempt and the figure seemed to solidify somewhat. *Danny? Can you hear me at all? Danny, it's Dad. Danny?* The figure turned its head side to side as if searching for something. Scott thought he saw its lips move. He drew more power from Brandon and tried again. *DANNY! DANNY...CAN YOU HEAR ME?* The figure turned its head in his direction and finally became recognizable as his son, although somewhat translucent. Scott could hear a faint voice and tried to draw still more power. DANNY?

The figure firmed up a bit more and Scott heard a distant voice. *Dad? Is that really you? I can't believe....*

Scott felt his concentration slipping, and the figure faded. He tried several more times, but exhaustion forced him to give up. He barely managed a weak, *Goodbye for now Lisa.* Before the connection faded.

He held his head in his hands, and Brandon called out concernedly, "Scott? Are you alright?"

Scott winced. "Yeah, I'm okay...got quite a headache, though. Well, thanks to you, I think I made contact." Rubbing his temples. "Maybe we can try again tomorrow."

Brandon nodded. "Sure, whatever you need Scott."

CHAPTER
Fourteen

LISA OPENED HER EYES TO SEE HER SON SMILING WITH TEARS running down his face. "I...I heard him. I SAW him, Mom. It was Dad! It was really Dad! To be honest, I didn't believe you, but...It was really him!" Wiping his eyes, he looked at his mother with a face full of wonder. "Where...where is he? What happened? We all thought he died with Mr. Higgins when that place exploded. What's going on? How is this possible?"

She sighed. "I don't really understand it myself, but... well, you know my psychic, Maria?"

Danny's eyebrows shot up. "You're kidding! She's... she's REAL!"

"Well, kind of. Your father had sent me a dream message, and then one day when Maria was trying to contact him...she actually did!" She laughed. "She didn't know she was real either, or at least she didn't know she could do that! Ever since then, your father has been talking to me quite a bit." She frowned. "He did say it makes him tired, though, so I'm not sure when he'll be able to do this again."

"But...WHERE is he? If he isn't dead, then what DID happen?"

Lisa sighed. "He said he's in a different world, where magic actually works. This young magician was really afraid of something and in a panic, accidentally summoned your father." She rubbed her chin. "It had something to do with all that electricity at that place, and the storm, and the lightning, and I guess there was a storm at the other place too, so they aren't sure exactly how it happened." Brightening she said, "But he's safe, and he says they will keep looking for a way to send him back."

Danny said slowly, "It sounds like a really cool place."

With a chuckle, his mother replied, "I guess it does."

~⁀ↄC⁀~

RONN TRACKER WAS IRRITATED. THE SUPPOSEDLY FOOLPROOF plan had not only failed, but failed badly. *I should skin that arrogant, useless magician alive!* he thought furiously. He looked in disgust at the tube in his hand. *Never fails, my ass! I'll show HIM something that never fails!* After hefting a slender, extremely sharp knife for a moment, he snarled and resheathed it. The only bright spot in this whole mess was that it was clearly Jons' magic that had failed. He strode down the hall and knocked on the door at the end.

"Enter," called a deceptively calm voice. Taking a deep breath, Ronn opened the door, and entered. "I'm sorry to say, sir, that this magic tube of Jons' did NOT live up to expectations. It failed to work on the primary target. This resulted in the capture of several hirelings, who admittedly were expendable, but one of them had one of the magic tubes, which is now in the hands of the enemy."

"So, they know the plan now?"

"They probably guessed part of it, but Greta was the only one who knew anything, and she was able to escape. The ones captured were simply street thugs who knew nothing."

"Well, that is something anyway," the man behind the desk responded evenly. "However, the operation DID fail, and the men you chose DID lose an expensive magic item." He held out his hand.

With a sigh, Ronn passed over a handful of gold coins. As much as he hated losing the money, it was well worth it to maintain the good will of this man. "Shall I attempt something a little more...direct, shall we say?" he asked carefully.

"What do you think the chances of success would be?"

"At the moment, they will be on their guard. Perhaps I can come up with something, though"

"Please do." Ronn stood up to leave. "And, Ronn...." Ronn turned and Makara went on quietly, "See if you can come up with something that will actually work this time. Dismissed."

～つC～

SCOTT HAD SLEPT LATE THAT MORNING. WHEN HE FINALLY shuffled bleary eyed into the workroom, it was nearly lunchtime. "How come nobody woke me up earlier?"

Morgan said grumpily, "Brandon told me about last night, and I just didn't want an exhausted person stumbling around my workroom." He muttered to himself briefly while mixing something, then continued, "We got a message relayed from Varney at Landbelow." He handed Scott a piece of folded paper. Scott unfolded it and began to read.

Things are slightly awkward at Landbelow right now. There are persistent rumors about Martin's incompetence, bad habits, etc. You get the idea. They keep trying to get me to interrogate people for them and act as their 'human lie detector'. They don't seem to understand that this would make me very uncomfortable, but such is life, I suppose. They are trying to hide the fact that they are having more and more trouble getting enough spare parts and there are also a lot of repairs that they are unable to make for themselves. Someone else would probably have asked for Scott's help before this, but either out of pride, or maybe resentment, they are obviously reluctant to do so. Perhaps they will reconsider if things don't improve. In the meantime, except for that, things are going well. I will keep you posted of any real problems to the best of my ability.

Varney

Scott refolded the paper and handed it back. "Maybe I should...." He stopped himself. "No, I guess I can't go there unless they ask, or have some other good reason, can I?"

Morgan grunted. "No. It would look like either interference, or as if you were favoring them over us, depending on who wanted to take offense at it."

Scott snorted. "Yeah, I can see that. People can be ridiculous sometimes." He frowned. "If we really wanted to go there, we could always say we need more...crap... no we can't."

Morgan looked at him. "Not really, not without letting more people know about the importance of the crystals, and I don't think that would be a good idea. Maybe someday...." he ended somewhat wistfully.

"Yeah, it would be nice not to have to tiptoe around

and hide what we can do." Scott sighed. "I think I'm going to go show John and Karg how bolas work. They may eventually come in handy."

Morgan nodded. "Yes, there certainly are times when it's good to be able to stop someone from running away without hurting them too badly." He finished with his mixing, and poured some of it into a small skin. "Would you mind delivering this to Fredo on your way past?"

"Sure, what's wrong now?"

Morgan smiled. "Nothing, for a change. They're going to be grilling some steaks, and I promised them a batch of my secret marinade."

"Oh! Sure thing."

After dropping off the marinade with Fredo's cook, *She really didn't seem too happy to get it. I hope she isn't too insulted.* Scott proceeded to a hillside overlooking the vineyard to demonstrate how bolas worked to his two guards, John and Karg. It went surprisingly well, and by the end of the day, all three of them felt reasonably comfortable with the new weapon.

"This would have come in quite handy a few days ago," John mused. "Thanks Scott, this was a great idea." He replaced the bola in the small bag that they had decided to carry them in. The others followed suit, and they left, Scott having been summoned to the castle for a brief discussion about the situation in Landbelow.

"Ah, Scott. Come in, come in." Count Wesley, ruler of Enimnori, was in a good mood. "So what's this I hear about our friends needing more help?"

Scott cleared his throat. "Well, they most likely could use some help, but don't want to ask for it. Morgan thinks, and I agree, that it wouldn't look good for me to show up uninvited, so I don't think there is really much that can be done right now."

"Yes, I can see that. So how are you, Morgan and young Brandon getting along? Any problems? Anything I need to know about?"

"No, we all get along pretty well, and I would say that things are going fine at the moment."

"Good, good." The Count sobered slightly. "Now, I'm sorry about these rumors going around, but I wouldn't worry about it too much, not that there is a lot that could be done anyway. For what it's worth, I certainly know you aren't a drunk, and anyone who really knows you knows it, too. If you are able to trace any of this nonsense, be sure to let me know so I can take the appropriate steps." He smiled. "Is there anything else I should know?"

Scott hesitated. "Well, it isn't a change or anything, but the Minthars contacted me again and said that the Klackaris are most definitely going whole hog into the mining business, and have discarded any thoughts of bothering with slaves."

Wesley looked amused. "Whole hog...I like that. It somehow creates a very graphic image, doesn't it? I guess that's all then. Please give my regards to everyone." As Scott left, he heard Count Wesley chuckle to himself, as he repeated "whole hog" while shaking his head in amusement.

When he got back to the workroom, Brandon was just finishing a project. "Hey, Brandon. How did it go?"

"Oh, alright. It wasn't that important anyway. You have that look on your face...what's up with you?"

Scott smiled. "I have an idea that I'm going to need help testing."

As he explained, Brandon's eyes grew round, and he said, "I'm not so sure that's such a good idea. You want me to shoot you with the crossbow to see if you can slow it down and make it miss? You're sure you're feeling alright?"

"Not AT me, past me. It should be safe enough. I'm going to try and use a little magic to slow it down."

Brandon said, "Do you have any idea what Morgan would say? I think the words 'moronic' and 'foolish' would be part of it. You aren't even wearing a helmet! What if I miss?"

Scott replied, "We clamp it on the table like before. I'll tell you what... I'll try it from...say...6 feet away to start with."

"I suppose, as long as it's clamped down, it should be safe." Brandon took the crossbow over to one of the workbenches and got some wooden clamps to hold it in place while Scott went to stand on the other side of the room.

The first few times Brandon shot the crossbow, Scott just watched, marked where the bolt hit and gave the bolt back to Brandon to reload. He smiled to himself, thinking, *I'm glad we set up that target. I don't think Morgan would appreciate a bunch of holes in the wall.* "Okay, that's good. I just needed a benchmark to test the results."

Brandon nodded, as he reloaded again. "Okay. Ready?" He waited while Scott made a couple of small gestures, then receiving a nod pulled the trigger again. The bolt sank less deeply into the target and was also slightly to the side. After several more shots with similar results, Scott rubbed his hands together and said, "Now, on to phase two," and stepped closer to the target.

"Uh, Scott. You never really told me what phase two is," Brandon said cautiously.

"I'll show you. Just gimme a second here." Stepping to within about a foot of where the bolts had been hitting, Scott quickly cast two spells and nodded. Brandon fired. His jaw dropped when, just before the bolt hit the target, Scott's hand shot out, and he snatched it out of the air. He tossed it back to Brandon and called out. "Again!" Brandon somewhat reluctantly reloaded and fired, with the same result. Scott smiled happily. "I wasn't sure that was going to work. Now I just have to set up a 'quick spell' for that combination and I will feel a little bit safer."

Brandon wrinkled his forehead. "Quick spell?" he asked.

Scott smiled. "Uh, yeah, that's something Morgan started helping me with a little while ago. You kind of pre-cast the spell, but don't trigger it. Then when it's needed it only takes either a word, or a small gesture to set it off. Of course, you can only...uh...hold a few at a time, and they only hold for a week or so, but, it's still kind of cool. I had read about something like that in a fantasy novel a couple of times and asked him about it." Frowning slightly, he said "He didn't act shocked or anything, so I just kind of assumed it was common."

Brandon started laughing. "I think both he and I have stopped being shocked by your...um...shall we say, 'innovative', ideas quite a while ago. You just think so differently sometimes, we either had to get...hardened to it, or walk around confused all the time."

Scott chuckled. "I guess I can understand that."

Brandon sobered a bit. "What did you do anyway?"

"Well, it's three spells, actually. One to slow down the projectile, one to deflect it, and another one to enhance my reflexes. The first two just have a small effect, and my reflexes are pretty good anyway. So it doesn't take much in the way of magic strength, just really careful control."

Brandon sighed. "So, just like your throwing thing, I may not be able to do this?"

Scott shrugged. "All we can do is try."

Brandon thought about it and said slowly, "Maybe not right now. I'm not sure if it would work for me anyway." He gave a dramatic sigh. "Now if you could come up with a better way of cooling fish eggs...."

Scott blinked. "Well, actually I might be able to come up with something." He frowned. "Yeah, give me a day or two to think about it...."

It took about three days for Scott to come up with some sketches. He cleared his throat and addressed the two in front of him, thinking to himself, *I'm glad Morgan was nearby. I probably would have had to talk to him about this anyway.* "Well, this should work, but it may take even more power than the ice trick, which, by the way, is how my people used to keep things cold until we discovered this."

Brandon said, "Wait, I thought you said your people didn't have magic. How did they make the ice?"

Scott chuckled. "Sorry for the misunderstanding. They would cut it from a frozen lake or something."

"Oh, so how does this work?" Both Brandon and Morgan were looking at the sketches. Morgan spoke first. "This looks very complicated. I'll need at least SOME understanding of what's happening." He looked at Scott expectantly.

Scott took a breath. "Okay, um…you know that when you compress something it heats up?"

Brandon looked confused, but Morgan nodded. "Yes."

"And also that when something evaporates it sucks in energy? Which it gives back when it condenses?"

Again, Morgan nodded assent.

"Okay, the idea is that this thing here," pointing to one of the sketches, "Compresses and condenses what's inside the system into the coils on this side which causes them to get hot. Then this set of valves basically sprays it slowly into the other set of coils, reducing the pressure, evaporating it and making them cool off. These two fans blow the hot air in one direction, and the cold air in the other. If you put the cold side into a sealed wagon, or room, then it gets cooler. Flip it around, and it can be used as a heater."

Morgan peered at the drawings for a while. "Okay, I think I understand. Is there anything else I need to know?"

Scott scratched his head. "Well, water is going to drip out of the cold side, other than that, I don't think so."

Brandon said curiously, "Why would it drip water?"

Scott said carefully, "The air can hold less water when it's cold."

"Um...OH! Okay, I get it, thanks Scott."

"You're welcome, Brandon."

"Now, first we have to decide what material we're going to use, and then talk about the power source. I know I've smelled ammonia around here before, so maybe we can use that to start with." Pausing briefly, Scott went on, "I'm not sure how to supply continuous power. My people use electricity, but I don't know if that's a viable option. Brandon, Morgan, can magic supply a source of power for long periods of time without exhausting somebody?"

Morgan considered this for a moment. "I think I read something about a device that will store magical energy. I'll have to do some research to see if it's practical, though."

Late the next morning, Brandon came to the workroom to find Scott sitting in a chair next to a wooden box a few inches wide about a foot long. "Good morning, Scott. What's in the box?"

Scott chuckled. "Just air."

Brandon looked at him curiously. "Um, is it okay if I take the top off and look?"

"Sure, go ahead."

Brandon removed the top, somewhat suspiciously, and looked inside. "It's empty."

Scott smiled. "No. it's not. It's full of air. I'm testing something."

Brandon sighed heavily. "Okay. What are you testing with a box full of air? And why is there ice on one side?"

Scott stood up quickly. "There is? That was quick!" He looked down at the now open box, and inserted his hand, moving it slowly back and forth. Cool!" he said triumphantly.

"What does that mean?"

"This end of the box is cool."

Brandon put his hand in the box and also moved from one end to the other. "Um…yeah, the end with the ice is colder. Were you finally able to create ice? I know you had some trouble with that before."

Scott smiled even more broadly. "Not exactly. I'm not sure how to explain it in your language, but I made it so the heat would collect at one end of the box, and make the other side cold."

Brandon looked at the box again. "But…there's nothing separating the two parts of the box."

"Well, there sort of is. There is a…." Scott frowned. "Okay, when you lowered the air pressure around those guys that were going to attack Morgan's house that time, you created a kind of barrier to keep the lower pressure area separate from the rest of the air…."

"No, I didn't."

"You had to, even if you weren't aware of it. Anyway, I did sort of the same thing inside the box. There is an… uh…invisible wall that only lets air through in one direction or the other depending on how fast the air molecules are moving."

Brandon held up his hand. "Wait. What are mahcules?"

he asked, obviously struggling with the unfamiliar English word.

"Well, do you remember what atoms are?"

"No. Something about being really tiny?"

Scott hesitated. "Well, for now, let's just say that everything is composed of tiny things that are always moving around a little bit. We detect faster movement as being hotter.

Brandon scratched his head. "I'm not going to be able to do this, am I?"

Scott said quickly, "I wouldn't say that. And what you do works well enough anyway. Now, if you would put the top back on the box, I want to see how cold this will get before it stops. I just wish I had a thermometer," he added wistfully.

Brandon smiled. "Can't you just invent one?"

Scott rolled his eyes. "Well, maybe, but not in time to help me with this." He looked at the box again. "Well, I'm actually surprised that it works. Now, I just need a way to control it so it doesn't go too far."

Brandon said slowly, "What could happen? Even if the box freezes solid, a little ice won't hurt anything."

Scott snorted. "Well, there is cold and then there is VERY cold. If it gets cold enough, the air will freeze."

"What? How could the air freeze?" He waved his hand around. "Air is just air. Isn't it?"

With a smile, Scott said gently, "Just about anything can freeze if you get it cold enough. For example, I've seen a demonstration where someone tapped a supercooled piece of steel, and it shattered like glass."

"What's glass?"

"Oh, that's right. I keep forgetting you people don't have glass. It's something that breaks very easily, at least unless it's specially made." He frowned slightly. "Someday we're going to have to explore the water's edge somewhere and see if we can find some sand and make some glass."

Brandon shuddered. "I don't feel like drowning, thank you."

Scott chuckled. "I'm sure we can...." his voice trailed off, and his eyes went distant as he felt a sudden chill. *What the heck is this? This feels like... My family, it has to be my family!* "BRANDON!"

Brandon startled, said sharply. "What?"

"Something is wrong with my family...I can feel it. Help me contact Lisa, then get both of our amplifiers set up in tandem. HURRY!" Brandon unlocked the cabinet, and carefully took out the two amplifiers that they had made. Leaving Morgan's inside, he placed them carefully one behind the other on the table in front of him.

Scott forced himself to take several deep, cleansing breaths before mentally reaching out. *LISA, what's wrong?*

SCOTT, Scott! We're in trouble, there's a forest fire, everyone else is gone, but the camper stalled, and I can't get it started!

You are still at the same campground?

Yes, the kids are in the camper with me. We can smell the smoke, Scotty, I'm scared. The wind is blowing this way, and I don't know what to... OH MY GOD! I CAN SEE IT!

Scott was suddenly overcome with a cold alertness. He knew what he had to do. *Lisa, calm down. I...we are going to try and bring you all here. Get the children as close to you as you can, then all of you concentrate on me and wanting to come here! I'll be 'back' in a moment.*

He dropped the connection to his wife and reached out with his mind. *MORGAN! MY FAMILY IS IN DANGER. I HAVE TO DO SOMETHING...WE ARE IN THE WORKROOM.*

<confusion> <shock>...then... I'm COMING!

Scott turned back to Brandon, his face cold and emotionless and spoke in a voice gone deathly calm. "Are you ready?"

Brandon looked at his friend fearfully. He swallowed nervously. "Scott? What is it? Ready for what? WHAT'S WRONG?"

"My family is in immediate danger," Scott stated flatly. "We're bringing them here."

Brandon straightened, the fear on his face being replaced by determination and resolve. He carefully checked the arrangement on the table, and focusing on his crystal, took several deep breaths and said evenly, "Ready."

Scott held up the hand wearing his wedding ring and now holding his crystal. He carefully filled his mind with the thought of his family in danger. Unbidden, he flashed back to the parking lot so long ago...two men laughing as they stalked the young woman cowering in fear. THIS time, instead of suppressing the anger, he focused on it, fed it, and let it grow. His mind filled with rage. *HOW DARE THEY!* He felt the rush of adrenaline, and the power surging and bellowing toward him from the amplifier.

Sensing the vast energy of a raging forest fire, he somehow drew on that as well. He channeled it…ALL of it into one single thought. *SAVE MY FAMILY!* The room seemed to waver. He heard the crackle of flames and smelled the choking stench of burning trees. He felt the growing heat on his face. He *REACHED OUT*…The room spun and blackness descended.

Epilogue

MARIA MONTENEGRO, DRESSED IN ALL OF HER FORTUNE telling finery, was getting ready for her first client of the day. She was carefully repositioning the pack of tarot cards when the glass ball in front of her suddenly seemed to pulsate. Her eyes widened, and she sat down heavily. Taking a deep breath, she closed her eyes. After a moment she began to smile. A short time later she opened her eyes. Still smiling she said softly, "Be well Lisa. I'm glad you are all safe and I hope you enjoy your new life."

Character list and locations

LOCATIONS:

Enimnori: City devoted largely to its ironworks, situated on the west side of one of few passes through the Green Mountain chain, guarded by Enimnori castle, ruled by Count Wesley and an advisory council

Sraj: Trading city, friends with Enimnori. Well known as a supplier of fresh fruits and vegetables, etc.

Dener Peak: a mountain far to the east of Enimnori. This is the location of the cave that is the only known source of magic enhancing crustal, and the location of the power interface betwee Landbelow and the derelict asteroid ship.

Landbelow: An underground complex/city near Dener Peak that contains the remnants of the former high-tech civilization.

Dead Lake: Site of the former "high-tech" city. Near Dener Peak, destroyed by nuclear weapons.

S'mark village: a small village inhabited by the equivalent of the Amish people. Unfortunate target of the Klackari slave sampling raid.

Lotipac: The capital city of the entire Enimori area.

PEOPLE:
OUR WORLD

Scott Hathaway: Manager/tech person at an electronics store. Expert in martial arts, active participant in a medieval reenactment group (SNARK)

Lisa Hathaway: Scott's wife, New Age enthusiast, co-owner/instructor at a Yoga studio.

Gwendolyn Hathaway: Scott's daughter age 14

Daniel Hathaway: Scott's son age 16

Frank Higgins: Deceased, worked at an experimental high-voltage electrical facility (friend of the Hathaways)

Rebecca Higgins: Frank's wife

Dr. Tom Johnson: Lisa Hathaway's therapist

Maria Montenegro: Lisa's psychic

Alta May Foote Platt: Lisa's mother, a wealthy socialite

Alston Hartwell Platt: Lisa's father, a semi retired M.D.

Susan Blackwell: Lisa's long time friend and business partner (at the Yoga studio)

VARUSHNA (THE PLANET SCOTT WAS SUMMONED TO)
ENIMNORI AREA

Brandon: A young, very powerful magician studying under master magician Morgan.

Morgan: Brandon's master and friend, an older, very skilled magician, owner/operator of the family vineyard/winery

Harold: Morgan's brother, career diplomat, very well connected

Babbette: Harold's wife

Varney: A strong mage, friend of Morgan

Valtir: another mage friend of Morgan

Fredo: old friend and neighbor of Morgan. Manages the day to day operations for Morgan's vineyard, Ineffectual (except or running the vineyard), clueless and somewhat slovenly, has a needy sister who "married well" and loves the "high society" of the area near the capital. She is a drama queen and Fredo lives in fear of having to assume responsibility for her if something happens to her somewhat sickly husband.

Burtha: Fredo's wife

Frannie: Fredo's cook (and housekeeper?)

Don: one of Fredo's grandchildren, age 16 ish

Mary: one of Don's siblings

Gertrude: Fredo's "very high maintenance" sister

Edgar: husband of Fredo's sister. Seems to be accident prone and in somewhat poor health. Fredo lives in terror of him dying and then having to take care of his needy sister.

Marta: a caravan worker/guard, friend of Brandon

Scott's guards: day, John, Karg, night: Graham, George

Brandon's guards: day: Cletus, Barl, night: Donal, Arn

Dormick: deceased former Baron of the greater Enimnori area, died mysteriously.

Harkness: New Baron, Dormick's replacement (after having Dormick killed), now deceased.

Makara: General, close associate of Baron Harkness

Jorgen: a lieutenant in Makata's army

Wesley: Count, rules Enimnori, and owns the nearby castle

Armis: leader of the Enimnori military forces, cousin of Count Wesley

Barton: caravan leader

Clem: The fourth member of the "village rescue" team. Chosen partly because he grew up in a nearby village and might be able to calm the captives somewhat.

King: un-named, only vague references

Don: blacksmith at S'mark village (first to report the mass kidnaping to Morgan, et. al.)

LANDBELOW:

Geon Mason: Scout at Landbelow, now junior ambassador to Enimnori

Ernset Chemiston: friend of Geon Mason

Martin Dener: leader of the 'resistance' at Landbelow, charismatic, autocratic, somewhat narrow-minded, wants to 'preserve the peace'

Franz Serif: Leader of Landbelow, with aspirations of ruling the world, xenophobic, autocratic, intolerant, somewhat sociopathic

John Steel: Franz Serif's 2nd in cmd

Winston Zedimore: friend of and 2nd in cmd to Martin Dener

Aliens
Klackari (the "pirates")

Alod-Boi-Gazaree: worker class-communications tech
Alod-ben-grsch: admin class-communications officer
Alod-bar-gaz: leader class-ship's 1st officer
Zarn-bar-maar: leader class-captain of the "ship Finder-of-Spoils. One of the few crew members not of the Alod family.

Minthar (the friendly empaths)

Mish349: communications tech, one of the few Minthars gifted with inter-species telepathy
Hensch661: In charge of Inter-species first contact
Jern811: Petty officer, equipment tech
Tkent412: Landing craft commander

About the Author

A former software engineer who grew up in Richmond, Massachusetts, Jeff is now retired and lives with his wife and mother-in-law in Western Massachusetts. He has four grown children, one son and three daughters, all of whom still reside in Massachusetts. He has a B.S. in Mathematics and has done graduate work in both applied math and computer science. An avid reader (mostly science fiction and fantasy) since grade school, he has now switched from printed to eBooks. His first novel was a long time in the making (nearly 20 years) and has been split into two books (Enimnori:Arrival and Enimnori: Discovery). Book three (Enimnori:Challenge) is now obviously complete, with book four (Enimnori:Crisis) expected in 2024.

If you enjoyed this book, please consider leaving a review on Amazon. Thanks in advance.

Any comments, questions, etc.? Feel free to contact me.
EnimnoriBooks@gmail.com
Or
Facebook.com/EnimnoriBooks

Books by Jeff Webber

Enimnori:Arrival

Enimnori:Discovery

Enimnori:Challenge *

Enimnori:Crisis (2024)

Preview of book 4

ENIMNORI: CRISIS

PROLOGUE

THE MITHAR SHIP DRIFTING IN THE TRAILING TROJAN POINT of the small moon noted the arrival of yet another huge mining ship, many of which were already drifting near said moon. Apparently the Klackari, who had been persuaded that mining the mineral rich moons would be more profitable and less trouble than taking the inhabitants of the planet and selling them as slaves, had taken their mining operations to a new extreme.

The captain of the Minthar ship was upset. Telepathically contacting her science officer, she asked, *How many mining companies?*

78, 12 more enroute.

<shock> Impossible! Her tentacles rippled in shock.

Verified.

Long term effects?

<worry>Unknown.

<frustration>Can be stopped?

Unknown.

Planetary tidal effect changes?

Probability estimate greater than 90%

Timing?

Uncertain..15 to 30 local years with 85% certainty

Effect on planetary civilization?

<fear><anger>Uncertain...variable count high. Tailings also being ejected into decaying orbits.

Impact hazards?

Minimal, debris size small.

Damaging heat result?

Uncertain...variable count high The science officer replied, beak grinding in frustration.

<anger><frustration>Notify Central...ask for legal precedent check. Inform Scott-human when Central responds.

<agreement>Yes sir!

~つC~

WINSTON ZEDIMORE WAS VERY CONCERNED AS HE ENTERED the office of Martin Dener, current leader of the small remnant of a formerly flourishing technological society, now residing in the decaying remains of a large underground facility. "Martin...I have more disturbing reports from the reclamation facilities and hydroponics levels." He handed a sheaf of papers to his friend. "Reclamation has needed several minor repairs, and is currently running in a degraded capacity due to a lack of spare parts. One of the hydroponics levels is only running at 70% and they aren't even sure why yet. We've lost another dozen light tubes during the last week alone, and the populace is starting to notice."

Martin took the stack of papers and began to look through them carefully. A short while later he looked up, his face drawn. "We're going to have to ask for help from the Enimnori people, specifically Scott, aren't we?"

He received a reluctant nod in response. "They are going to keep trying, but, yes I'm afraid it looks that way."

"Have we searched the empty areas of both Home and the Entrance Facility?"

"Yes, but we have assigned different teams to look again. Maybe the others missed something."

"But you don't think so, do you?"

Winston sighed heavily. "No, I don't."

Looking at the paper again, Martin scowled. "Alright, keep me posted. How long do they estimate before this becomes critical?"

Winston looked down. "They wouldn't commit themselves. When I asked privately, some of them thought it would be a matter of months, but most said several years at least." He spread his hands helplessly.

"Very well, be sure to let me know if anything significant happens."

Printed in the USA
CPSIA information can be obtained
at www.ICGtesting.com
JSHW010337090923
48052JS00014B/382